PRAISE FOR MAGICKEEPERS: THE ETERNAL HOURGLASS

"This fantasy earns style points for being set in modern Las Vegas—in a hotel whose residents include polar bears, giant Siberian tigers, and Princess Anastasia herself...A pleaser for fans of Michael Scott's Secrets of the Immortal Nicholas Flamel series."

—*Kirkus*

"This is a fun action story, moving quickly and easily through adventures and magic...which helps reluctant readers."

—*Library Media Connection*

"The intricate, well-paced plot...feels plenty original, and kids will be charmed by [Kirov's] brand of magic."

—*Publishers Weekly*

"Exotic locale, unusual characters, weird food, polar bears, tigers, magic, and a thirteen-year-old boy suddenly discovering he is part of a Russian magical dynasty. Yes, fans of fantasy and history will be pleased with this new series by Erica Kirov..."

—*School Library Journal* blog

"This book is so well thought through that I am beginning to think that Erica Kirov may actually be from a family of magicians. I have been bewitched and I can't wait for book two. A *vonderful* novel!"

—Children's Book Review

"Incorporating famous figures from the past such as Rasputin and Houdini, this book is an exciting introduction to Nick's magical family and their quest to restore the magical elements that have been lost to them."

—Young Adult Books Central

"As the core of the adventure unfolds, the author seamlessly blends facts and folklore of Russian history and historical figures in the world of magic with her modern-day story."

—Reading Tub

"*Magickeepers: The Eternal Hourglass* is simply amazing. This is a story of great imagination, magic, and the power to believe in oneself. For lovers of Harry Potter, this new series by Erica Kirov is sure to be a huge hit."

—Café of Dreams

"I found it a delightful escape into imagination and intrigue."

—Dolce Bellezza

"Kids will love these books because they are fun and funny…and parents will love the fact that their kids are learning something (there's a lot of history from Tsarist Russia in this book). Parents will also appreciate the fact that their kids are reading and are enjoying it…If you know a young reader (anyone from about eight or nine on up, I would say), get them this book. But be prepared to get them the rest of the series, too, because they will be hooked."

—Blogcritics

MAGICKEEPERS

THE
PYRAMID
OF SOULS
BOOK TWO

MAGICKEEPERS

THE PYRAMID OF SOULS
BOOK TWO

ERICA KIROV

Magic is more than an illusion

sourcebooks
jabberwocky

Published by Sourcebooks Jabberwocky, an imprint of Sourcebooks, Inc.
P.O. Box 4410, Naperville, Illinois 60567-4410
(630) 961-3900
Fax: (630) 961-2168
www.jabberwockykids.com

Library of Congress Cataloging-in-Publication Data

Kirov, Erica.
  Magickeepers : the pyramid of souls / by Erica Kirov.
    p. cm.
  Summary: Thirteen-year-old Nick Rostov and his large, extended family of Russian Magickeepers continue to battle the evil Shadowkeepers, who now seek a miniature pyramid of souls that once belonged to Edgar Allan Poe.
  [1. Magic—Fiction. 2. Magicians—Fiction. 3. Good and evil—Fiction. 4. Families—Fiction. 5. Poe, Edgar Allan, 1809–1849—Fiction. 6. Las Vegas (Nev.)—Fiction.] I. Title. II. Title: Pyramid of souls.
  PZ7.K6382Map 2010
  [Fic]—dc22

                            2009049936

Source of Production: Berryville Graphics, Berryville, Virginia, USA
Date of Production: May 2010
Run Number: 12241

To my children

ACKNOWLEDGMENTS

I would like to thank all of the children in my life, including those I have met while visiting classrooms. A very special thank you to Becky Mills, an extraordinary teacher. Your support of the book is very special. A shout-out to Mrs. Mills's class of 2008–2009. You guys totally rock. I hope middle school is being kind to each of you and that you will always be certain of the magic you store inside your hearts.

I cannot possibly name all the kids who have written to me and those who are my friends, but…a few names: Tyler, Zachary, Tori, Cassidy, Pannos, Eva, Sofia, the gang from New Hope—you all know who you are. A special acknowledgment to Lauren (who always lets me know how excited she is when she is reading my books), Miranda (who got to be a character!), and of course, especially my friend Jacob P., who was the first kid I let see the galleys of Magickeepers Book 1.

To my agent, Jay Poynor, who has always been my biggest fan and supporter. To Lyron Bennett, who first embraced the Magickeepers, and now to Daniel Ehrenhaft—his enthusiasm has been so terrific. An *enormous* thank you to the staff at Sourcebooks Jabberwocky. I feel like I am in author heaven with you guys—from the team that pulled together the incredible cover, to those who painstakingly edited the manuscript, to Heather Moore in publicity. Dominique Raccah has assembled one of the best teams in the publishing universe.

To my best friend, Pammie, for being a beacon of support to me. Last, but never least, to my children, Alexa, Nicholas, Isabella, and Jack, who provide me with so much inspiration, in particular for this series…but also, quite simply, in life.

All that we see or seem is but a dream within a dream.
—Edgar Allan Poe

Magic is believing in yourself. If you can do that,
you can make anything happen.
—Johann Wolfgang von Goethe

Dream no small dream; it lacks magic. Dream large.
Then make the dream real.
—Donald Wills Douglas

CONTENTS

PROLOGUE

Spring Garden District, Philadelphia, Pennsylvania, 1844

E DGAR ALLAN POE SAT AT HIS WOODEN DESK AND STARED OUT the window at the starless midnight sky. His jumbled study reflected the scattered state of his mind. Books competed for space on shelves and had tumbled to the floor in small piles, their spines cracking. A lantern burned, its flames creating a flickering glow on the plain white walls.

His wife, Virginia, was in the small back bedroom, coughing in her sleep. Consumption was ravaging her health, and Poe was even more desperate now for success. He was weary of fighting for every penny, every scrap of recognition. Though he'd made a living—barely—as a literary critic, he longed for success as a writer. He needed a poem or short story that would capture the imagination of both an editor and the nation: one that would make him wealthy, famous, and able to care for Virginia.

But inspiration would not come.

He stared down at the paper, quill pen in his hand. The white page taunted him with its blankness. He clutched his temples, urging words to spring into his mind…then reached for the snifter on his desk. He took a deep, long swallow of amber cognac. More than he cared to admit, his inspiration flowed from the burning liquid—but tonight, the muse did not come.

And if not now, then…would the muse ever?

"Please," he whispered desperately; it was almost a prayer. "Inspiration. That is what I need."

From the back bedroom, he heard Virginia's rattling cough. He felt as if his own lungs shuddered. He winced, then dropped his head in his hands, anguish etched in his pale face.

Tat-tat-tat.

Poe jumped nearly out of his skin at the sound. He stared at the cognac bottle. Its color was so alluring, like a jewel. Was he now having hallucinations?

But then he heard the sound again.

Something was at the window.

He felt a tingle, as if a cockroach skittered up his spine, and then a chill filled him with dread. How could something be at the window? He was on the second floor.

Shaking, he stood and crept toward the panes of glass, peering out into the darkness. He wondered if a tree branch could have broken free from the oak across the way.

Tat-tat!

It was a more insistent sound. The pecking of a beak.

Squinting in the lamplight, Poe cautiously opened the window. A large, black bird stared at him inquisitively from the sill. Blinking twice, it stepped in and alighted on the floor. Poe's heart thudded in his chest. The bird was not small. With its head erect, turning in nearly a full circle atop its neck, the bird easily stood taller than his knees.

"Once upon a midnight dreary," the bird spoke in a voice as clear as Poe's own.

Poe blinked. *That voice!* It was deep, familiar…but entirely alien at the same time. He took three steps backward and fell into a chair.

"I *am* hallucinating," he muttered to himself.

"Nothing of the sort," the bird replied. "I am here to bring you your deepest desire."

"A raven…to answer my deepest desire? How do you propose that?" Poe asked. He scarcely believed he was talking to a bird, still half-certain it was all a dream or a bad batch of cognac.

"My name is Miranda. I have come as an answer to your prayer. Write down what I say, and you will be rewarded."

Poe stared. *Miranda.* Her beak was ebony and forbidding. Its point appeared dagger-sharp.

"Your pen. Begin writing," the bird insisted. She took several hops and preened her feathers, which shone like mica in the lamplight. She spread her wings, blocking the light, casting Poe in shadows.

Poe returned to his desk, still not certain of anything—including his own sanity. He dipped his quill in ink and began copying down the raven's words.

"While I nodded, nearly napping..." the bird spoke. Her voice was throaty, clear, and haunting.

Poe scribbled as the bird dictated.

"But the raven still beguiling all my sad soul into smiling..." She flitted and hopped toward the long-cold fireplace. The log Poe had burned was now nothing more than ash.

"What this grim, ungainly, ghastly, gaunt, and ominous bird of yore...meant in croaking 'Nevermore.'"

As Poe wrote down "Nevermore," he felt a spark of recognition. *Nevermore*...sounded precisely like a raven's autumnal call. *Brilliant!* he thought.

The bird continued, "'Is there—*is* there balm in Gilead?—tell me—tell me, I implore!' Quoth the raven, 'Nevermore.'"

As if in a trance, Poe continued to write, terrified that he might miss a perfect word of this gem-like utterance, this masterful poem.

"'Take thy beak from out my heart, and take thy form from off my door!' Quoth the raven, 'Nevermore.'"

Poe gasped as the poem started to draw to a close. "And

my soul from out that shadow that lies floating on the floor...
shall be lifted—nevermore!"

When the bird was finally done speaking, Poe stared down
at eighteen stanzas of poetry, six lines each. It was perfection—
the greatest poem he had ever written, even if the words filling
the previously blank page weren't his own creation.

"That poem shall make you famous, Edgar Allan Poe," the
raven said proudly. She stretched her wings and shook her
tail feathers.

"Why have you come to me?" Poe whispered, uncon-
sciously turning toward the room where his wife lay
coughing. His eyes flashed back over the poem, still
marveling at its genius.

Miranda flew and landed on his desk. Her eyes shone like
two black diamonds.

"In exchange for this poem, someday I shall return to you and
ask you for a favor. You may not refuse me, Edgar Allan Poe,
or you will experience ruin and death. Is that understood?"

"But what kind of favor?" Poe asked.

"A magical favor. I may need you to hold something for
me—for safekeeping. From forces you cannot understand.
Forces nearly as old as sand and time. Shadows."

Poe swallowed. Could this bargain be worth it? But there,
staring at him, were the words on the paper, so magnificent.
He thought of his life, moving from city to city for jobs as

an editor, begging for money from benefactors so he could write or keep afloat the literary magazines he worked so hard to create. These words were worth any bargain. Surely they were.

But then he felt that reptilian chill again.

From the back bedroom, Virginia coughed once more—a rattling sound, as if she'd begun to drown. Poe winced. Just that afternoon, she'd coughed into a lacy handkerchief, and spots of blood had formed an ominous pattern.

Sweating, frightened, and desperate, he nodded at the bird. "We have a deal."

"Do you swear it? On your honor and word as a gentleman?"

"I swear it," Poe breathed, his voice hollow.

"Excellent," spoke the raven.

Outside, a fierce wind rose up from nowhere, filling the room and rustling Poe's books and papers.

"They are near," the bird whispered. She took flight and soared out the window, her call echoing through the night. "They are near! They are near! Nevermore! Nevermore!"

Edgar Allan Poe ran to the window and shut it, locking it in fear for his life.

He returned to his desk, sweating nervously despite the cold air. What kind of deal had he just made? Had his bargain been struck with the forces of evil? Had he gone mad? A bird with supernatural powers...

He pulled his silver pocket watch from his vest pocket and pressed the fob. The watch opened, revealing a photo of Virginia and a small lock of her hair.

"I would do anything for you, my love," he whispered. "I always will."

But what would it cost him?

SPECIAL DELIVERY

O N THE VERY TOP FLOOR OF THE WINTER PALACE HOTEL and Casino, Nick Rostov and his younger cousin Isabella sat on his immense four-poster bed playing cards at midnight—long past both their bedtimes. Isabella rested her head on her enormous Siberian tiger, Sascha, as if the ferociously huge yet tame cat was a furry pillow. The tiger purred as loud as an outboard motor.

"Come on, Nick," Isabella chided him. "Your turn!"

The two cousins were playing Magic Eights. It was like Crazy Eights, only the cards sometimes spoke to them—or heckled them was more like it.

"So you don't have a queen *or* a diamond?" The queen of diamonds, dressed in an Elizabethan costume, rolled her pale blue eyes and folded her arms across her tiny chest.

Nick kept drawing cards from the deck and finally slapped a two of diamonds on top of the queen. "That'll shut her up," he said.

"Not likely, young man," a muffled voice squeaked from beneath the top card.

Suddenly, there was a knock from the inside of Nick's closet.

Isabella grinned at Nick and clapped her hands. "Pizza's here! I'm famished."

Nick climbed off his bed and opened the ornately carved closet door with the family crest etched in real gold in the center. Crazy Sergei stepped out, holding a pizza. The top of the box read, *Crazy Sergei's Impossibly Great Pizza Pie*, and a cartoon drawing of Sergei decorated the box—wild black hair and furry caterpillar eyebrows included.

"Here you go, Nick!" Sergei's voice boomed. Sergei had three volumes to his voice: loud, *louder*, and LOUDEST.

"Shh!" Nick held a finger to his lips. "Do you want him to hear you?"

"Who? Damian?" Sergei asked. He was, as usual, dressed in a traditional Russian folk shirt of brilliant red—with intricate embroidery sewn down the front and around his collar—black pants, and black leather boots polished to a glossy sheen.

"Yes, Damian," Nick snapped.

A few months before, on the night of his thirteenth birthday,

Nick had been kidnapped from his bedroom by his cousin Damian—the most famous magician in the world. Nick hadn't even known he *had* a cousin—*any* cousins. Before then, ever since his mother had died, he and his dad had lived alone in hotels where his dad worked. Most recently, they stayed in the Pendragon, a drab little hotel in the older part of town with worn carpeting and an even more worn showgirl revue. Nick had been planning a summer of skateboarding (more specifically, perfecting the nightmare flip), junk food, and blissful, couch-potato, lazy goodness. But Nick soon discovered he was actually related to an entire enormous and magical family of Russian magicians—*real* magicians, not illusionists.

With a snap of his fingers, Damian had literally whisked Nicholas to live on the top floors of the glamorous Winter Palace Hotel and Casino, and the magic was *real*. From levitation to mystical swords that flew through the air to closets that opened for pizza delivery, Nick discovered that his family hid its magical abilities by performing as a magic act. No one in the audience had any idea when Damian pierced a beautiful woman with a sword and turned her into a dove that he was actually really doing it.

The world of their magical clan was exciting. In school with his tutor, Theo, Nick had learned how to make his pet hedgehog disappear and how to create fireballs in the palms of his hands. But Nick had also learned that Damian—Theo's brother, and the leader of the family because of his incredibly powerful abilities—preferred that everything, from the food they all ate to the clothes they wore, was Russian, to reflect their ancestry. *Their destiny*, Damian was always saying. Pizza, Damian declared, was off-limits. Contraband. But Sergei offered almost anything—for a price.

Sergei lifted the lid of the pizza box. The crust was perfectly browned, the mozzarella cheese melted just so and gooey. The pie was slathered with pepperoni.

Nick's mouth watered. "Oh, man…awesome."

"This is not just any pizza pie. It's *Brooklyn* pizza pie. And you may not know it, but that means it's the best pie in the world. You couldn't even make a *magic* pie as good as this one. I had to cross time zones to get it here still hot."

"Thanks, Sergei." Nick handed him a crisp twenty.

"By the way, if Damian finds out you ordered pizza, you didn't get it from me," Sergei said.

"Your name's on the box," Nick scoffed.

"Hmm…" Sergei waved his hand and a black pen appeared in it. He crossed out *Crazy Sergei* on top of the box and wrote *Crazy Tony*.

Nick shook his head. "Oh sure, Sergei. That'll fool him. The most famous and brilliant magician in the world won't be able to figure out it came from you."

"Well, then make the box disappear when you're finished.

I've got to go," Sergei said. "I'm working on a deal to bring an entire trio of trained lions to another act."

"Is there anything you won't sell?" Nick asked Sergei, who usually dealt in exotic animals but had lately branched out into the pizza and Chinese food delivery business, too.

Sergei raised his bushy eyebrows. "I do not think so, Nick. Well, I wouldn't sell a pizza to Damian. But that's about it."

Nick took the pizza, and Sergei retreated back into the closet and shut the door. Nick couldn't resist opening the door again and peering inside. Sergei was gone. Only Nick's clothes—and his costumes for the magic show—hung on the rod, perfectly pressed.

"Midnight snack," Nick said, shutting the closet door and setting the pizza down on the bed.

Isabella rubbed her stomach. "I can't wait. I'm *starving*. I can't believe I only had my first taste of pizza when you came here. I have to make up for all my pizza-less years!"

His cousin bit into a slice and then picked off a piece of pepperoni and tossed it in the air. Sascha caught the pepperoni on her impossibly huge, wide, pink tongue and then swallowed it.

"I didn't know tigers ate pizza," said Nick.

Isabella shrugged. "Not usually, of course. But I can't eat in front of her and not even offer. I think she likes pepperoni. She also seems to have a taste for jellybeans and caviar." She paused and smirked. "Hey, if I win, Sascha gets your last piece, okay?"

"We'll see," Nick said with a pretend serious gaze.

Before they could even pick up their cards again, there was a bumping in his closet. Nick rolled his eyes.

"Bet you anything that Sergei wants to sell me something else," he said to Isabella. "It would be just like him to show up with one of his animals. Yesterday, he had some scheme to train spider monkeys as card dealers for the casino. Like Damian would ever go for that!"

"Indeed not," came the muffled voice of the queen of spades.

Nick stood and opened the closet door—and Damian emerged—all six feet, two inches, and haughty blue eyes.

"Pizza?" Damian's eyes flashed angrily. "Card games?" He stared at Nick's bed, covered with chattering cards, all nervously whispering, "Damian's here! Damian's here!"

Nick spread his hands out wide (and he hoped innocently). "So? We're just hanging out."

"Need I remind you, young cousins, that you have important exams coming up? And you should be preparing for the convention, not eating questionable food from that parasitic little Sergei. Wait until I get my hands on him." Damian snapped his fingers. "I may just turn him into a flea on a pig's behind if he doesn't watch his step."

"Honest, Damian," Nick said, "we're ready for our exams."

"Really? So you've mastered levitation?"

"Sure. Of course I have."

"So if I take you to the roof and casually toss you off of it, you would manage to safely levitate your way back to the roof rather than becoming a flattened little pancake on the sidewalk below?"

"Why do you always have to put everything like that? Doom and gloom and death and destruction?"

Damian peered down at Nick and then Isabella. "The two of you should know precisely why. You almost lost your *lives* to the Shadowkeepers. You nearly drowned in the polar bear's pool, not to mention the battle in the desert. This is no time for pizza and card playing." He glanced at Nick's skateboard leaning up against the wall. "Or skateboards, with your flips and slides. You must be studying! Ready for battle at a moment's notice! Ready to fulfill your destiny!"

Damian turned to go, opening the door to the closet. "One more hand of cards. One more slice. Then off you go, Isabella. You both need to get your sleep to be ready for your studies first thing in the morning." He winked at them and then disappeared, vanishing in the blink of Nick's eye.

"That's progress, you know," Isabella said after a moment.

"What do you mean?"

"There was a time when Damian would have simply made

the pizza and cards disappear *and* yelled at us. He *did* say we could have one more slice."

They played another hand of Magic Eights—Isabella won and tossed Nick's last piece right into Sascha's mouth.

"Hey!" Nick cried, laughing. "Rematch tomorrow."

"If we do…we'll have to be careful not to get caught. Maybe no pizza."

Nick smiled crookedly. "Sorry, Isabella…it's just not cards without pizza."

Sascha appeared to nod in agreement. Then the big cat stretched luxuriously and yawned, licking her chops.

"I know, precious. Time to go to sleep." Isabella stood. "Good-night, Nick." She left his room, Sascha padding behind her like a kitten trailing after its mother.

Nick changed into his pajamas and settled into bed. His room was enormous. Most of the things in it had belonged to his mother: ornate Fabergé eggs encrusted with gold, folksy wooden boxes painted with brightly colored birds and stylized black stallions, and a fancy silver brush and comb set. He had no memory of her, really, but he liked having her things around him. Since settling in, he had also tried to make the room a little more like his own. Tony Hawk posters competed with images of Russian life.

His room had no television and no video games. Damian forbade it. Nick had a radio, but if he turned it on, the only music he could get was Russian, and unless he felt like listening to a *volynka*—a Russian bagpipe that was Damian's favorite instrument—Nick had learned to keep the radio off.

However, he had inherited a special gift—aside from the ability to do magic—from his mother. He could Gaze. His crystal ball sat on his dresser, and by concentrating hard, Nick could make television appear in it—another no-no in Damian's book.

He leaned back on his pillow and watched MTV. His stomach was full of pizza, and it was making him sleepy. Life in the luxury hotel was pretty fun. He and the entire family performed an incredible magic act each night—of course, the audience never guessed it was all real magic. Each night—and twice on Saturday, when there was a matinee—the audience wildly applauded as he cast his spells. School was taught by his cousin Theo and mostly consisted of learning magic and history. He hadn't had to do long division since he'd arrived! (Which was a good thing considering his math grades.) And all his essays were on the Tsars—Russia's kings and queens of old. Now that Sergei was in the pizza business, life was just about perfect.

His dad and grandfather had even moved into the hotel on the first floor. Aside from his mom, he had everything: his new family; his dad and Grandpa; and he even had a skate-board ramp in the basement. Damian didn't know, but Nick was teaching the bellhops how to ride long boards.

Nick switched channels on his crystal ball just by thinking it. On the late news, the anchor said, "Convention time here in Las Vegas. This is when out-of-state visitors flock to the many conventions for every profession and interest you can think of."

Nick laughed to himself. No one in the real world would guess what was happening in the secret, hidden magic world. In two weeks, a magical convention was being held at the Winter Palace Hotel and Casino. Magic families from all over the globe, disguised as hundreds of accountants, would descend on the hotel. He would meet magicians from places like Tibet and Japan and Greece—and, of course, Egypt.

According to Theo, all magicians had their roots in ancient Egypt. Their history was embedded in the great pyramids, in the Sphinx, in the desert itself—the timeless yet shifting sand. Magicians were revered at that time. They didn't have to hide their gifts. But eventually, Theo said, people persecuted what they did not understand. Magicians scattered, hiding in plain sight. The Salem witch trials were some of the most famous persecutions. Over centuries, each branch of the original bloodline created its own new bloodline. They rarely saw each other. Nick tried to imagine an entire hotel filled with other magicians. He couldn't wait.

He rolled over on his side. When he shut his eyes, his mind flashed. He bolted upright in bed and clutched his temples. He was used to having visions—he was a Gazer, and that meant he could see the past, the present, and the future. But his visions hurt when they had to do with the Shadowkeepers: those magicians from the dark side, also as old as the ancient sands.

Nick squeezed his eyes shut, trying to see with his mind, but all he saw was darkness. Then, in the next instant, a crowded ballroom, filled with magicians. Then more blackness, spreading like an oil spill.

His head continued pounding. He opened his eyes, but the room spun dizzily like the Tilt-o-Whirl at a carnival. The Shadowkeepers couldn't be planning on coming to the convention. They wouldn't be that bold after he and Damian and Theo had defeated them in the Nevada desert months ago. Surely, they would stay away.

But as he slid back down underneath his covers, he already knew. The Shadowkeepers were not only that bold—they were that evil.

And they would stop at nothing to destroy him and his newfound family.

THE GREATEST SHOW ON EARTH

*T*HE NEXT MORNING, NICK VISITED MASLOW IN HIS STALL. His majestic horse was kept with the other animals behind a high stone wall at the back of the casino (hidden from paparazzi and pesky journalists). His giant Akhal-Teke's coat shimmered like fourteen-karat gold.

"Hey, Maslow," Nick said, holding out a perfectly ripe Macintosh apple. The horse nibbled it from Nick's palm and whinnied his approval. Suddenly, Nick felt two heavy paws on his back. He stepped forward and whipped around. Sascha and Isabella stood there, grinning. At least, Nick thought the Siberian tiger was grinning. He could see her long, pointed, shining white teeth.

"Have you heard?" Isabella asked.

"Heard what?"

"Damian has secured an elephant for our show. I am going to ride in on her back, and you get to make us *both* disappear."

Nick rolled his eyes. "I don't see what was wrong with the old show. Why does he insist on creating an entirely new show every few months? No other casino in all of Las Vegas does that. Shows usually last for years."

"He likes the challenge," Isabella said. "You know him. He gets bored."

"Yes, but *his* being bored means *I* have to learn a whole new act—all new magic, everything."

"Which is as it should be." Their cousin and tutor, Theo, approached the stables, his long, black scholarly robes swirling behind him. He stood very tall, like his brother Damian, with jet-black hair cropped very close to his head, high cheekbones—a familial trait—and eyes with the bluish tint of a glacier.

"Of course, you'd defend him," Nick mumbled. "He's your brother." *And he bosses us all around,* he thought.

"You are too impetuous, Kolya," Theo scolded, using Nick's Russian nickname. "You should know by now that Damian lives to protect his family. The reason he changes the act has nothing to do with boredom." Theo adjusted his horn-rimmed glasses on his nose and turned his gaze to Isabella, who flushed.

"Then why?" she asked.

"To keep our skills sharp. Think of it as training. Each new feat increases your power. It deepens your skills as magicians. Plus, Isabella, you know there is a competition at the convention."

"A competition?" Nick asked.

Theo nodded. "Each clan will perform magic onstage, and the winner is declared by a measure of applause. We have never lost."

"Never?"

Theo shook his head. "Никогда. *Never*. This year, however, we hear rumors of a Parisian contingent with a very unusual display of magic. We want to be sure we win."

"Is there a prize?"

Isabella said, "The winner can choose any act of magic and claim it."

"Claim it? What do you mean?" Nick asked, as Maslow leaned his head down and pushed on Nick's hand, looking for another apple. The horse stamped his hoof in disapproval and shook his luxurious forelock.

"Each family has secrets belonging only to them," Isabella said. Sascha leaned up against her.

"We have," Theo said, "for example, our snow. While other magicians may try to replicate the snow that falls on the casino…we have perfected it. Our crystalline flakes are real. If one should land in your hand, you would see that it is precise and perfect. I hear that a magical tribe in Kenya once tried to create snow as a respite from the heat but succeeded in making only hail."

"So if we win, we are gifted with the secret of a single feat of another clan's magic. Anything we want. That is how Damian obtained that French guillotine that can behead a man and then magically piece him together again. We also win bragging rights," Isabella added. "After all, when Damian puts on his billboards that he is the greatest magician in the entire world, it is completely true."

Nick sheepishly kicked at the hay in the stall. "It's not that I don't like learning new magic. It's just that I was getting comfortable with the old act. It's a lot to remember! And I'm not so good at memorizing."

"I know. I grade your Russian vocabulary tests! But no worrying. And no sulking!" Theo commanded. "Come, meet Penelope."

"Who's that?" Nick asked.

"My elephant," Isabella said. "Come along."

Nick followed his cousin, watching her long ponytail swing across her back. She was now his best friend, but he had learned three things about her. One: she was bossy. Two: she thought she knew everything. And three: all the animals were hers—and she let him know it. She and her older sister Irina were magical in their own way—they could communicate and control even the wildest and most dangerous of animals with spells that only the two of them and the women of their lineage knew.

Isabella and Sascha turned a corner, with Nick and Theo close behind. Nick stopped in his tracks. Rising above him was the most enormous elephant he had ever seen in his life—she was on her two hind legs, trunk in the air, and ears spread out like wings.

"Penelope," Isabella commanded, "you may curtsy. This is Nick—the one I told you about."

Penelope lowered her trunk and returned to all four feet with a thud that rattled the ground. Then she appeared to actually curtsy, bowing low until her trunk swept the floor.

"She looks—I don't know...ancient. Wise," said Nick. Penelope's eyes were ebony with gray lashes framing them, and she wore a headdress and halter with faceted jewels that glittered in the sunlight. "Like she knows something I don't."

"She *is* very wise," Isabella answered. "She's ancient. And magical. P. T. Barnum wanted her for his circus."

"Really?"

Theo nodded. "After the death of Jumbo."

"Jumbo?"

"P. T. Barnum was the first man to have a traveling circus. He had human...'oddities,' they called them. Like Cheng and Eng—'Siamese' twins. And a little person named Tom

Thumb. And an elephant named Jumbo. The elephant died in a train accident—and Barnum sought a new elephant."

"I'm about to get a history lesson, aren't I?"

Theo nodded with a wry grin. "Penelope here has a special crystal ball."

Nick was used to Gazing. He had his own crystal ball, but once he got good at Gazing, he didn't always even need it. The crystal's power communicated to him in his mind. But Isabella couldn't Gaze, so for history lessons, they would peer into crystals from Theo's crystal ball collection, viewing history as it unfolded.

Theo pushed back Penelope's ear. The elephant's magnificent jeweled harness wound around her head, encrusted with pink and purple stones. From the top of the elephant's headdress dangled what looked like a purple jewel the size of a large melon, but now Nick could see that it was actually a crystal ball.

Penelope bent her head and Theo waved his hand. The purple orb filled with smoke.

"Behold," Theo said, "Penelope...and the greatest show on Earth!" He winked at Nick. "Until us, of course."

✧　✧　✧

Waldemere Mansion, Bridgeport, Connecticut, May 1883
P. T. Barnum, wearing a black suit, starched white shirt, and black bow tie, surveyed the enormous elephant that

stood—incongruously—in his backyard. His thick, dark hair was filled with strands of silver, and he patted the elephant's trunk.

"She's magnificent. I must have her." He looked down at his dear friend, General Tom Thumb. "Don't you think she would be a fine addition to our circus?"

Thumb crossed his arms and nodded. "Indeed," he piped up in a nasal-sounding voice, quite booming for his size.

A man with a thick Russian accent shook his head. "I do not think so, Mr. Barnum."

"But when we met at the court of Tsar Alexander II, you assured me you would have oddities for my museum," Barnum protested. "You even showed me some of the collection in the possession of the Tsar, the *Kunstkammer*. Remember that entire display of pickled punks!"

"You may have the pickled punks. But this elephant...she knows secrets."

Barnum motioned for Tom Thumb. "Look...do you think this elephant knows secrets?"

The tiny man, just over three feet tall, motioned for the elephant to lower her trunk. The elephant's trunk formed a *U* and Thumb sat on it, like a swing. The elephant lifted her trunk until General Tom Thumb stared right into her ebony eyes. Thumb looked down at Barnum. "Indeed. This elephant knows secrets. Ancient secrets. We must have this elephant."

The elephant lowered the little man to the ground, and he hopped off her trunk.

"I trust Tom Thumb to make many of my business decisions. He has saved me from financial ruin more than once! We will pay whatever you ask," Barnum said to the Russian.

"I'm afraid that is impossible. Instead…I will offer you a dancing bear."

"I already have a dancing bear. And one that can ride a bicycle. We need an elephant. Jumbo had been our star attraction. The circus is not the same without an elephant."

"How about a wager?" the Russian said, a twinkle in his eyes.

"What kind of wager?" asked General Tom Thumb, squinting his eyes and studying the Russian.

"If I can make this elephant disappear before your very eyes, you will give me the magnificent crystal ball from the fortune teller in your circus—the one on display in your front hall."

"And if you can't?" said Barnum, staring at the sheer size of the large gray elephant.

"Then you shall have the elephant."

Barnum looked at Tom Thumb. "What say you, Tom?"

"Deal," said the little man. "The wager is on."

"Fine," said the Russian, his eyes a pale, almost icy blue. "Fetch the crystal ball then."

P. T. Barnum walked into his magnificent Victorian mansion and returned to the yard with the crystal ball. It was as large as the standing globe in his study and so heavy that his knees bowed from the effort.

"Here," Barnum grunted, handing the ball over. "But I believe you have made a sucker's bet. This crystal ball is nothing but glass. And I shall soon own an elephant even bigger than Jumbo was! America will clamor to come see my circus."

The Russian man nodded. "So you think, Mr. Barnum." He walked around the elephant three times, then whispered something in the elephant's ear. He spoke words—Russian words—so quickly that it was impossible to discern them. Then he clapped his hands three times.

In an instant, the elephant, the Russian, *and* the crystal ball were gone.

And P. T. Barnum and General Tom Thumb stared, mouths agape, at the yard where the elephant had just been. The grass was even tamped down in huge circles where the elephant's feet had been. P. T. Barnum scratched his head. "Well, I'll be a monkey's uncle," he said. Then the greatest showman on Earth started laughing, a loud, delighted, uproarious sound that came up from his belly.

"Tom…I believe we've been had!" he exclaimed. And the two old friends chuckled, walking around the yard, clearly trying to fathom how the Russian had performed such an amazing feat.

✦ ✦ ✦

"Is that elephant—the one in the crystal—is that Penelope?" Nick asked. "That would make her really, really old."

"Indeed," said Theo. "And she still holds onto her secrets. And now you, like your ancestor before you, will make her disappear. Just like that."

"Sure," Nick said. He had made his hedgehog, Vladimir, disappear. But he had also lost his little pet for an entire night once when he couldn't bring him back from wherever it was that things went to when they disappeared. Vladimir was chubby, but still weighed less than a pound. In Nick's mind, all he could think was, *How am I going to make something that huge disappear?*

"I can read your mind, cousin," said Theo. "After lunch, we will begin preparations. For this will be our greatest show on Earth."

NEWTON'S FOURTH LAW

*L*UNCH WAS A TYPICAL FEAST WITH HIS EXTENDED FAMILY. It was held in the dining room around a massive gleaming table so long that one hundred people could eat at once beneath a glittering chandelier. Tigers stood watch over them, and ornate silver samovars floated through the air, pouring steaming cups of bitter black tea. But the food… was gross. Nick had his choice: borscht, that dark red beet soup—beets!—or stewed cabbage, which smelled like gym socks. Nick ate bread. Lots of bread.

After lunch, Nick started down the hall to class. As he walked, he felt a shadow fall across the window, darkening the hallway.

Normally, snow was the only thing Nick saw out the windows of the top floors where the family lived. The Winter

Palace Hotel and Casino, though it stood in the arid, dry heat of Las Vegas, had a perpetual snowfall over it, meant to remind the family of its "mother country" of Russia. The snow was cold, white, and bright and glistened in the desert sun. Daytime in the hallway was impossibly light. But there, in the midst of the swirling snowflakes, flapped the largest black bird Nick had ever seen.

Nick took a deep breath and froze. Slowly, he inched closer to the window. He pressed his nose to the glass, and the bird flew closer, staring right at him, its black eyes shiny as buttons.

Nick swallowed hard. It was a crow, or maybe a raven with a black beak, and Nick could only assume a bird as large and dark as that must belong to one of the Shadowkeepers. He stepped backward and then rushed down the hall to Theo's classroom.

Bursting into the room, he was about to tell his older cousin about the black bird, but he stopped himself before he could blurt out the words. If he told Theo about the bird, the entire family would snap into overprotective mode. No more pizza from Sergei. No more lazy dips in the pool with the polar bears. No more Magic Eights. No more riding his skateboard in the basement, far from Damian's prying eyes. No more fun. No more anything but sword fighting practice and school, school, and more school. He was just starting to get used to life with the family. He'd wait. He'd wait and see just what the appearance of the mysterious black bird meant.

Nick slid into his seat next to Isabella. Theo tapped the face of his watch. "You are late, Nicholai."

With that, the cuckoo clock on the wall ticked loudly, and a bird emerged, squawking, "Late, indeed! Late, indeed!" It flapped its wings and ducked back into the clock.

"Sorry, Theo."

"Young cousin, there is much to learn in a short amount of time. Now, just how are you going to make an elephant disappear?"

Nick shrugged. "I guess the same way that I make Vladimir disappear," he said, thinking about his pet hedgehog. That first horrible time he lost poor Vlad, he'd felt like a failure. But he had become better with time and training. He just wasn't so sure he wanted to try to make an ancient elephant disappear—in front of an audience of three thousand people. And with Damian demanding perfection!

Theo took off his horned-rimmed glasses and rubbed them on the black robes he wore nearly all the time.

"When you make Vladimir disappear, is it exactly the same as making Sascha disappear?"

Nick shrugged.

"Think about it. *Exactly* the same?"

Nick shut his eyes and thought about it. What did making something disappear feel like? He usually felt a strange sensation in the pit of his stomach, and his arms tingled—in the same way that they sometimes did when he could feel the electricity in the air before a thunderstorm. Then he usually felt a surge, an indescribable force hurtling through him. His temples always throbbed, and then he imagined the magic—what he wanted to happen. He pictured it in his head, and then when he opened his eyes again, whatever he wanted to disappear was gone.

"Yes. Exactly the same."

Theo put his glasses down on the desk. He waved his hands, and Nick felt himself being lifted from his seat.

"What are you doing?" Nick asked. He tried to grab his chair, but he soon found himself suspended in midair.

"And now Isabella," Theo said.

Nick's cousin was soon in midair, too, only she started turning somersaults.

"Showoff," Nick muttered.

"Now…Isabella, you are light as a butterfly. And Kolya," Theo scolded, "you have been eating too much pizza." As Theo spoke, his left hand lowered, bringing Nick closer to the ground. His right hand—for Isabella—raised up, and she soon was touching the ceiling. "So no, it is not *exactly* the same. Not moving you in flight and not making you disappear."

He moved his hands, and Nick and Isabella were once again seated at their desks. "Now think, Nicholai. You know the true answer to this. Does it feel *exactly* the same when you make Vladimir disappear versus Sascha?"

At the mention of her name, the big cat lifted her head lazily.

Nick shut his eyes and tried to recall how it felt the first time he made his hedgehog disappear. Then he pictured the magic act at the precise moment when he had to transform Sascha into Isabella—and the big cat disappeared for just a moment or two. "Well, I guess now that you mention it, when I have to make Sascha disappear, I have to try harder. I can't explain it, really, but it's like the air is heavier."

"Precisely. So then how do you propose to make an *elephant* disappear?"

"I don't know." Nick sighed, grinning slightly. "Why do you always speak in riddles and questions? Why can't you just tell me?"

"I suppose we should start, my cousin, with a little instruction on the physics of disappearing into thin air."

"Physics? You do know I barely escaped sixth grade, right?"

"Perhaps," said Theo, "but we have a fabulous teacher at our disposal: one of the world's greatest magicians, Sir Isaac Newton."

Nick furrowed his brow. "Wasn't he the guy who discovered gravity? Like from a falling apple or something?"

Theo pointed a finger at a crystal ball—one of hundreds perched on pedestals around their classroom—along with potions and mice in golden cages. There were also all sorts of mysterious ingredients and creatures that glowed and moved in mason jars—everything from hairy spiders, purple crickets, and speckled frogs to whale milk and gleaming fluorescent goop that smelled like cauliflower. "The boy who got a C in science and an F in math. Why am I not surprised you think it was all about an apple?"

"You mean to tell me that one of the most famous guys in history was one of us? A Magickeeper?"

The crystal ball was now floating through the air and landed on Theo's desk. Inside, it turned pink, then grew darker and darker until it glowed ruby red—and then darker still until it looked like the crimson color of blood. "Time, cousins, for another history lesson."

"I was afraid of that," Nick sighed.

✩ ✩ ✩

Cambridge, England, July 5, 1687
Sir Isaac Newton sat at a wooden desk furiously scribbling with a quill pen, which he repeatedly dipped into a short, square bottle of black ink as dark as liquid mica. His assistant entered the room.

"Today, Professor Newton, is a day of great accomplishment," said the young assistant, dressed in clothes of the day, with a fancy ruffled shirt, cuffs and trousers that ballooned out, and a long coat. He grinned earnestly. "Today, your three laws of motion are published, and all the world will know of your genius."

"Indeed," said Newton. "*Lex I: Corpus omne perseverare in statu suo quiescendi vel movendi uniformiter in directum, nisi quatenus a viribus impressis cogitur statum illum mutare.* Every body persists in its state of being at rest or of moving uniformly straight forward, except insofar as it is compelled to change its state by force impressed."

"The law of inertia," said the assistant.

"Followed, of course, by the ideas of mass and velocity…and movement," Newton lifted a finger, "and reciprocal actions."

"The world will never be the same."

"Let us hope," muttered Newton, adjusting his white-powdered wig.

"May I bring you your supper? I see, by the papers on your desk, that you are hard at work."

A thick wax candle burned, and the room was cast in gray. Newton stood and looked out the window. "No. I haven't even touched my pot of tea from the afternoon." He casually waved to a silver tray laden with biscuits, jam, and a silver teapot perched next to a porcelain teacup. "My tea is quite cold now, I'm afraid."

"I can bring you a fresh pot!" his assistant said brightly. "Sir…I have never understood how so wise a man could forget to eat. This is the third untouched tray this week."

"No, no—don't bother. When I am hard at work, it seems I can scarcely remember to eat or drink. I am perfectly all right."

"If you change your mind, sir, I shall have the cook prepare you some cheese and meat, perhaps with a pudding."

"I will let you know if I require sustenance."

"Excellent, sir." Newton's assistant bowed. "I will leave you to your most important work." He turned and left Newton's library.

The famed mathematician waited until the door was shut. Then he turned from the window and the darkening sky. Smiling to himself, he lifted the paper where he had been writing. Though he had dipped his quill into the black ink, the words he scribbled disappeared, the letters seeming to melt away. And now, new words formed.

"My fourth law," Newton whispered. "If the third law is that for every action, there exists an equal and opposite reaction, the fourth law is that for every magical action, there exists, in the magical realm, an equal and opposite reaction."

Newton shut his eyes. In an instant, he disappeared, only to reappear several minutes later on the other side of the room. He laughed. Then he slapped his knee. "Ah, if the world only knew!"

He strode over to his desk and blew on the paper. Once again, the words rearranged themselves into black letters in formulas and scratched-out equations. The magical words were gone.

ELEPHANTS NEVER FORGET

$\mathcal{T}$ HEO'S LITTLE HISTORY LESSON DID NOTHING TO HELP NICK
understand how to make an elephant disappear. It only
confused him more. Sir Isaac Newton even had a magical
formula for making something disappear:

$$(n\lambda = 2d\sin\vartheta)a = \frac{4\text{pi}^{**}2r}{t^2K} = \frac{\frac{1}{2}V^{**}2 - G^*M}{r3.2616\text{ light years}(3)} \longrightarrow$$
$$\text{par sec } 299792458 \text{ m/s} (3e8).1\,10000010^\wedge \quad 410^\wedge 3\,(n\lambda = 2d\sin\vartheta)a = 4$$

$$\text{pi}^{**}\,\hat{F}_N(\hat{u}_\circ) = F_N(u_\circ) + F_N(\hat{u}_\circ)(u - \hat{u}_\circ)$$

Nick studied the intricate combination of figures, numbers,
and symbols that had been written by Isaac Newton in magic
ink. He stared at the formula. He tried to memorize it, but
that just gave him a massive headache—the kind he used to

get in math class, when he would feel like he was swimming under murky water. Nick didn't think learning magic was simply memorizing formulas or spells or magic words. He wished it were that simple, but he knew from his very first attempts at magic that it was more complicated than that.

Magic was emotional. Theo said it was rooted in the heart of a Magickeeper. It was in his blood, in what he believed, in what made him happy, and in what made him grieve. If Nick was angry, sometimes his magic worked more quickly, more powerfully. But if he was *too* angry, the opposite happened. Or his magic got sloppy. And if there was one thing Damian hated, it was sloppy magic.

Nick knew for sure that he was never going to be able to make an elephant disappear by studying Sir Isaac Newton's formula.

He would just have to find another way to make Penelope disappear.

✩   ✩   ✩

The stage lights shone on him so brightly that he had to squint. Nick's heart pounded. It was only a rehearsal, but just walking on the stage always made his pulse quicken.

Isabella rode in on Sascha, arms in the air, bareback. She grinned, looking as if she were riding a bicycle downhill and taking her hands off the handlebars, wind whipping through her long hair. The massive Siberian tiger pounced across the stage as if running after a tasty wild boar on the Siberian plains. Nick saw Sascha's muscles rippling, animating the thick, furry stripes. Then the tiger halted as it faced the elephant. Penelope rose up on her two hind legs and let out a deafening trumpet call that shook Nick's knees. She raised her trunk in the air, then danced nimbly on her hind legs as if she were a ballerina.

Not to be outdone, Sascha rose up on her hind legs as Isabella wrapped her arms around her tiger's throat. Sascha roared fiercely, showing off her gleaming pointed teeth.

Penelope, as if obeying the command of the tiger, then returned to all fours and slowly lowered herself toward the stage floor.

Together, as one, Sascha and Isabella leaped onto Penelope's back. Isabella climbed down from Sascha. The tiger then scampered down Penelope's back and landed on the stage floor on all four paws.

Isabella balanced on Penelope, pirouetting, before sitting astride the giant gray animal. She grabbed tight to the jeweled halter, which glittered brightly in the stage lights.

All eyes now turned to Nick. This part of the new show was supposed to be simple, according to Damian (whose definition of "simple" was usually a lot different from Nick's). All Nick had to do was levitate through the air, landing directly in front of Penelope and Isabella. Then he would make the two of them disappear before calling for Maslow, climbing on his horse, and galloping across the stage. Finally, he would act as if he had second thoughts about his decision, wave his hand, and bring elephant and girl back.

Nick stared deep into Penelope's eyes. *I can do this, I can do this...* he breathed to himself. He felt the familiar electricity inside him: butterflies in his stomach, only more fierce. *Bats* in his stomach, beating against his rib cage as if wanting to escape. In his mind, he pictured the magic exactly as he wanted it to happen. But then his thoughts flashed—a distraction—and all of a sudden, he saw the raven inside his head. He tried to shut out the picture, but when he tried to move Penelope with his magic, nothing happened. The elephant was a brick wall.

He opened his eyes. Penelope was staring at him, batting her lashes. Her eyes were enormous black globes, and now that he was face to face with her—or nose to trunk—he could see that General Tom Thumb had been right. Penelope's eyes seemed ancient, knowledgeable. As if she knew secrets going back to the dawn of time.

Isabella cleared her throat. "Ahem," she said, peering down at him expectantly.

He looked over his shoulder. Damian was scowling. Nick shut his eyes and tried again. He pushed with his mind. It almost hurt—like something punching him in the gut and knocking the breath out of him.

He decided to stop trying to do magic his way, because it wasn't working. *Sir Isaac Newton was a brilliant guy,* he thought to himself. *Maybe he knew a thing or two about magic.* So Nick instead tried to think of all those confusing numbers in Sir Isaac Newton's formula. The numbers and strange figures and symbols represented the elements of magic: time, space, power, joy, love, despair, triumph, loyalty, belief. In a way, they represented the very roots of the Magickeepers.

Nick tried to move Penelope once more. Again, his lungs shuddered; again, he felt an invisible punch. He inhaled and concentrated. Still, nothing happened.

When he opened his eyes, the hot breath of Penelope was blowing in his face through her trunk.

"Stop it!" he snapped and slapped away Penelope's trunk with his hands. "Come on, Penelope! Are you trying to embarrass me in from of everyone? Huh? Because I don't appreciate it. You have to feel me trying to move you, Penelope! You're not cooperating."

Behind him, Nick heard the familiar *click-click-click* of Damian's polished black boots as he strode forcefully across the stage floor.

"What seems to be the problem, little cousin?"

"Penelope is not budging!" Nick's cheeks reddened. He hated looking stupid in front of anyone—it felt like when he had to read in front of the class at his old school. But he especially hated not getting something right in front of Damian. His older cousin made magic look so easy, and he had no patience for anything in the show that was not done to perfection.

"And you think it's Penelope's fault?" Damian looked down his nose at Nick.

"Yes. Well…it feels like she's not letting me move her."

"That's silly," Isabella said from high atop the elephant.

Nick shut his eyes and sighed. "It's *not* silly. I can't explain it, but it feels like that elephant wants to make me look bad."

Isabella glared at him. "Stop talking about my elephant that way. You're being completely ridiculous."

"But I can feel Penelope resisting me. She's doing it on purpose, I swear!"

At that, the elephant blew into his face, dampening it with wet elephant spit that smelled of hay.

"Gross!" Nick yelled, wiping his cheeks.

"You deserve it!" Isabella called from high atop Penelope. "You're bullying her!"

"I'm sorry." He wished he could melt into the stage and disappear—but he hadn't learned how to do that yet.

Damian scowled at his cousin. "She weighs 11,000 pounds; perhaps you are not trying hard enough. Or your magic isn't strong enough. Perhaps we have put our faith in the wrong person, Kolya."

At that, he stamped his left foot and waved his hand, and Penelope and Isabella vanished. It was just like in the crystal ball with P. T. Barnum and General Tom Thumb. One minute, they were there, and the next…only air and the faint, lingering scent of hay.

"How did you do that?" Nick asked.

"By not offending Penelope."

"But—"

"An elephant never forgets. I suggest you practice more. No lazy magic. A little less pizza, a lot less card-playing, and a little more magic. And when Penelope and Isabella return… you should grovel for forgiveness. This was not Penelope's fault. Now off with you. I have no patience for you when you are ill-prepared for rehearsals."

"Ill-prepared!" Nick sputtered. "Ill-prepared?"

"Off with you!"

Nick stormed off the stage, cheeks still burning. He clomped to the back of the theater. Under the lights, Damian clapped his hands, and Isabella and Penelope—all 11,000 pounds of her—returned.

Nick sighed. Practice? Fine. Like all magic, he would study how to do it.

But practice?

Where was he going to find something that weighed 11,000 pounds to practice on?

MICE AND SHADOWS

ICK WALKED THROUGH THE LOBBY TO A DOOR WITH A LARGE *Do Not Enter! Employees Only!* sign. On the other side of the door was a very long, dark corridor. Precisely in the middle of the hall, two magical sconces immediately lit with flames shooting almost to the ceiling before they settled into candle-sized flickers.

Nick proceeded to the sconces and faced the wall. An elevator door, one that had blended perfectly with the wall, slid open. He stepped in. There were no buttons to push. The door shut, and with a *whoosh*, Nick was carried to the top floor of the hotel. He exited on the private family floor.

The hallway was empty and silent. No one was around. They were all in rehearsal, and he was alone. He felt a tingling up his spine, as if a spider was crawling up each of his vertebrae. His breath quickened, and he walked faster. Something didn't feel right.

Then he heard a *tap-tap-tapping* sound on one of the tall windows that lined the hall. He turned to face the glass, and there it was—the raven again, its malevolent blackness stark against the swirling snow.

He felt some inexplicable pull, as if its eyes, which studied him so intently, were also hypnotizing him. Nick tried to break the raven's gaze, but he couldn't. The raven seemed to know him—seemed to want to speak to him. He felt a physical tug, as if a black thread were weaving a dark bond between them.

He squinted at the bird as it hovered in the snow. He was growing weak. Finally, with all the strength he could muster, he imagined a pair of golden scissors slicing through the black thread. Then Nick turned his back, hurriedly opened the door to his room, and slammed it shut. As soon as he was safely inside, he walked to his crystal ball and placed his hands on it, hoping to Gaze. But the ball was cold. Its smooth surface was almost icy.

"Please," he whispered. "I need to know why that raven is here." Ordinarily, at his touch, the ball grew warm, then hot, and then filled with visions. Theo had taught him to bond with his crystal ball, to think of it constantly so that visions would come to him whether he was Gazing directly into the ball or not. He and his crystal ball were one. Usually. A panic settled inside him like a stone near his heart. What if the raven was a Shadowkeeper's minion, and it was draining his magical abilities? Then he wondered if Damian was right. What if, for some reason, his magic *wasn't* strong enough?

The Grand Duchess, the ancient woman who had faced down the evil leader of the Shadowkeepers when she was a little girl, had once told him that his magic was even stronger than Theo's and Damian's. He backed away from the crystal ball and sank down on his bed. The Grand Duchess had to be wrong. His magic was fading.

Nick frowned. He hadn't wanted to be a Magickeeper when he arrived. He had hated the food, the costumes, and the fact that his summer of couch-potato freedom had been stolen from him by Damian. But the magic itself had kept it from being unbearable, and now that he had gotten used to his life, he liked it. A lot. He liked snapping his fingers to make his bed. He liked looking into his crystal ball, summoning Crazy Sergei, and having pizza and sweet-and-sour chicken delivered through his closet. He liked having a cousin he got to do everything with. He still loved his dad and grandfather, but he was from more than a family of two now. He was from a clan, a huge family. And they loved him.

He had to get his Gazing powers back. He didn't want to return to his old life again. He bet that they would send him away. Unless he could move Penelope, they would send him back to the Pendragon—to being an ordinary kid with not-so-great grades, a tiny little room, and a life without magic.

"I don't want to be ordinary," he said aloud.

He fell onto his back and stared at the ceiling. *Caviar,* he thought to himself. It was the only thing he could do without. No matter how many different ways they served those salty little fish eggs, he hated them. Except for that, he needed the Winter Palace Hotel and Casino; he needed his new family. He was a Magickeeper. That empty feeling he'd had his whole life—of not belonging—had been replaced. This *was* home.

"Please." He spoke aloud, as if the entire line of Magickeepers before him could hear, like ghosts hovering near the ceiling. "Please don't let me fail."

He had never been good at anything but skateboarding. But ever since he'd come to live at the Winter Palace, he had started to believe deep down inside that he was good at something else…

A knock at the door interrupted his thoughts, startling him.

Nick bolted upright. What if it was the raven? Could ravens knock? But then he realized that in his crazy life with the family—of course, a raven could knock. And polar bears could take him swimming. And tigers ate pepperoni pizza…and jellybeans. Nick walked to his door and peered into the peephole.

"Great." He cringed. Isabella and Sascha. His cousin was probably going to yell at him some more.

He opened the door, ready for her to scream. "Go ahead, let me have it. I was a jerk."

"Let you have what?" she asked.

"You're going to yell. So get it over with."

"I'm angry with you, Nick, but we have more important problems right now."

"Yeah. Like the fact that I can't seem to budge you and that 11,000-pound elephant of yours."

"No. Bigger problems than that."

"Bigger problems than an 11,000-pound elephant?"

"Yes. This!" she said, and she thrust a squeaking white mouse at his face.

"A mouse?" Nick raised one eyebrow. "You're weird, but… this is nuts, even for you. This mouse is a big problem?"

"No. Not the mouse. What he's *seen*." She looked over her shoulder and tiptoed into his room with Sascha padding silently behind her. "Hush."

Sascha stretched out on the carpet in front of the door—she always guarded the door. Isabella walked over and set the little white mouse down in the middle of Nick's bed.

"If that mouse poops on my bed, Isabella, I swear—"

"Shh! Listen to him."

"Listen to him?"

"I said hush!" Isabella put her finger to her lips. She sat down gently on the bed and looked sincerely at the mouse. "Go on, my dear, sweet, little Pasha. Tell us what you know."

The mouse sat on its haunches and squeaked. It moved its paws and wriggled its nose, and its ears perked up. Isabella nodded sympathetically.

"Poor thing. You see?" she said to Nick. "I think that's the problem."

Nick shook his head, exasperated. "No, Isabella, I *don't* see. I don't speak mouse! You do."

Isabella giggled and then covered her mouth apologetically. "I sometimes forget. Just the other day, Irina and I had the most marvelous conversation with Vladimir."

Nick glanced over at his hedgehog. "Vlad never talks to me. He mostly clicks and huffs. And eats mealworms."

"That was something he expressed quite clearly. More mealworms, please! He also says you snore."

"Isabella," Nick said. "Focus! What did the mouse say? And am I really asking you about what a mouse—a little rodent—has to *say*?"

"Yes, you are. And it's important. You see, Pasha and his family live down in the stalls with the other animals. They sleep in the hay, and they share their food. Pasha, in particular, likes spending time with Penelope. They have become very good friends."

"I thought elephants were afraid of mice."

Isabella looked at Pasha, who fell back on the bed and grabbed his furry white belly. He appeared to be laughing. Nick's cousin smiled. "A silly little tale. Completely untrue."

"Well, how would I know that?"

"You might have simply asked. But anyway, Pasha says that in the evening, as most of the animals were sleeping, he happened to want a drink of water, and as he was scurrying through the stalls, he saw a Shadowkeeper. An enormous beast—the stench nearly caused him to faint. Worse, there was a black bird flying overhead, dark and sinister."

Nick felt all the air in his lungs rush out of him. He tried to swallow.

"What?" asked Isabella. "You look like you've seen a ghost."

"Not a ghost."

"What then?"

"What's worse than a ghost?"

"A Shadowkeeper?" Isabella whispered.

Nick nodded. "I have something to tell you. And you're not going to be happy with me. But you can't tell anyone else."

"I don't like the sound of that. Last time you asked me to keep a solemn secret, cross my heart and hope to die, I nearly *did* die in a desert."

"Please, Isabella. Just promise."

"All right. I promise."

"Cross your heart."

"Yes. Cross my heart. But I *don't* hope to die! Now tell me."

"A raven has been following me."

"What?" She leaped from the bed and grabbed Pasha. "Maybe that's why your magic powers are waning. The Shadowkeepers are coming." Her cheeks drained of color, and her pale eyes widened. "Nick…what if they come during the convention? There will be so many clans here, so many people. Every single room in the entire hotel is booked. What if they disguise themselves?"

"We'll *feel* their presence," Nick said. "When I'm near a Shadowkeeper, my skull pounds like someone is beating it with a hammer. And there's the stench."

Isabella wrinkled up her nose. "Yes, there is that."

"Their smell reminds me of the time this kid left his lunch bag with three hardboiled eggs and a tuna fish sandwich on the bus all day when it was ninety-eight degrees out. That afternoon, when we got back on, it was a barf-fest."

"I've never smelled that, but I'll take your word for it."

"My point is, they won't be undetected. If they come to the convention, they won't get away with it, Isabella."

"We need to tell Damian and Theo."

"No!" Nick said firmly. "Not yet. I don't want to run to them every time I see a shadow or a black bird. I don't want them to feel like they have to be overprotective of me. I want them to count on me. Besides, if we tell Damian and Theo, we'll be in lockdown. We won't be able to do anything."

Isabella bit her lip. "I would miss pizza. All right." She nodded slowly. "But at the very least, we must go get Pasha's family. I don't like thinking of the little mice down there. Sascha can take care of herself, and Penelope and the lions can, too. But mice? Come on!"

✧　✧　✧

By the time they reached the stalls, the sun was setting fast over the Las Vegas strip, and the lights were coming up. Nick always felt blissfully dizzy as the neon danced its crazy rhythms and illuminated the world, writhing in syncopated beats.

The two cousins slipped into the stalls with Sascha between them. Isabella set Pasha down, and they followed the scampering mouse as he wove through the legs of horses and around piles of hay until he arrived at a cozy little nest near Maslow's trough.

"Come here, my little angels," Isabella whispered, a tremor in her voice. She scooped up three baby mice, each just the size of her thumb, and handed them to Nick. Then she picked up Pasha and his wife, Dashia. "Come on," she urged Nick. "Let's go. Hurry!"

The two of them turned, and then Nick smelled it. "Please tell me that's like...elephant poop or something," he whispered.

Isabella bit her bottom lip and shook her head. "No. That's Shadowkeeper stench if I ever smelled it."

"Put the mice in your pocket in case we have to make a run for it," he whispered.

The two of them hurriedly tucked the mice away. Isabella put Pasha and Dashia into her jeans, one at each of her hips, peering out, trembling. Nick put the three baby mice in his shirt pocket, where they popped up and looked out, little black eyes wide with fear, noses twitching as they sniffed the air.

"Get down, babies," he urged them.

Maslow began kicking the hay in his stall, his snorts low and rumbling. Soon, the other animals grew agitated as well. Nick heard Penelope's trumpeting call. He grabbed Isabella's hand, and they backed up against his horse. "Maybe we should climb on Maslow and ride out of here."

But it was too late. Sawdust from the floor of the stall blew into their eyes, so Nick and Isabella ran around and hid behind Maslow. Nick patted his horse's neck and whispered in his ear, "Easy, boy. I know you remember."

Maslow was one of the rarest breeds of horses in the world, an Akhal-Teke. He was a magnificent, metallic gold, bred to race long distances. Theo had told Nick that the Russian horses, like Maslow, were known to race over two hundred miles across the plains without water. With Nick urging him on, Maslow had carried Nick and Isabella far into the Nevada desert, outrunning flying beasts in the night in the last showdown with the Shadowkeepers. Maslow had bravely stayed by their side as the evil monk Rasputin, the leader of the Shadowkeepers, had appeared, ready to kill them all. Maslow's muscles twitched. The horse clearly sensed a Shadowkeeper now.

Nick felt the tiny mice trembling in his pocket. His own head pounded. He rubbed his temples.

A large, black, foul-smelling shadow grew in size and cast the entire stall into pitch blackness. Nick whispered, "We're trapped in here."

The shadow swirled, forming a funnel like a tornado. It spun so fast that more sawdust and bits of hay flew up. Maslow reared on his hind legs. Nick could barely see; his eyes stung with dirt and dust.

"Ouch!" Isabella cried as sawdust flew at her face.

When the funnel stopped spinning, a Shadowkeeper stood six feet high, its wrinkled, leathery wings outstretched and encompassing the stall from one end to the other. Its face— once human, but now reptilian—was scaly, yet slick with ooze. Its noxious odor made Nick feel sick.

Maslow kicked his front hooves, rearing up and moving

toward the Shadowkeeper, causing the evil beast to back up a few paces. Sascha roared and charged, baring her teeth and inciting the other large cats to roar in solidarity.

Suddenly, a woman walked out from behind the Shadowkeeper. With jet black hair, a wide slash of a smile, and hideously garish red lips, she looked crazed. Yet something about her was very familiar—something about her eyes.

"Maria!" Isabella breathed.

"Who?"

"I know her."

"What?"

But there was no time to explain. Maria, whoever she was, pointed at them with a long talon of a finger, and—despite the tiger, despite Maslow—the Shadowkeeper edged toward them, hissing and squealing like a wounded, feral animal.

Then behind Maria, a black, wolf-like creature trotted up, fangs bared. It snarled and snapped, saliva dripping from its mouth and pooling on the ground. The beast looked very hungry. Its yellow eyes narrowed to slits, focusing on Nick and Isabella as if planning on making a meal of them. A growl rumbled deep in its throat.

Nick whispered, "Whatever that thing is, it's like it has rabies or something."

Suddenly, a hoarse *caw* echoed in the sky. Then there were hundreds of *caws*. Nick and Isabella looked up at the sky through the window of Maslow's stall, which was full of ravens, maybe thousands of them, their cackling calls all echoing across the night. They nearly blocked the lights of Las Vegas, flapping in a frightening, unified chorus of wings.

"What else can go wrong?" Nick asked.

"Look!" Isabella shouted.

The ravens seemed to frighten the Shadowkeeper. The beast drew back its wings, folding them into itself like a cockroach's wings. It moved out of the stall and hissed at the birds. With its sharp claws, it scraped emptily at the sky, like a zombie. Then it changed shape, melting into a slick, oily puddle which the wolf-like beast sniffed.

Maria pulled a necklace up over her head and opened a triangular vial hanging from the gold chain. The oil moved toward her. She set the vial down and the ebony liquid filled it. Then, glaring at them, she put the cap back on the vial and returned the chain to around her neck.

The wolf-like creature lunged toward Nick and Isabella. Maslow rose up on his hind legs and kicked out toward it. Maria emitted a low growl of her own, as if communicating with the beast. It drew back to her side, and together they vanished in a burst of black smoke.

The ravens, now a fluttering mass of darkness, flew higher and sped through the night, out toward the desolate desert that lay beyond the borders of Las Vegas.

Nick stared at Isabella, his heart pounding. "Who was she—and how do you know her?"

"She is my sworn enemy," said Isabella. She put her hand to her chest. "My heart is pounding." Her breath was shallow.

Nick frowned. His cousin was a know-it-all sometimes, but she was also the kindest person he'd ever met, protective of her family just as she was of her tiger (and of all animals). She wasn't the type of person who would have a sworn enemy.

"What are you talking about?" he asked.

Isabella shook her head. In the weakest of voices, she said, "Oh, Nick, I have to break my promise to you. This is very bad. Worse than I feared. So we have to tell the family."

LEGACY

*I*SABELLA SAT DOWN WITH NICK IN THE SCRATCHY HAY OF THE barn. Maslow lowered his head and nuzzled Nick's hair as if to make sure he was all right. The horse whinnied softly and twitched his tail.

"This all happened before you came to live with us, Nick. Before you were born. Before I was born. You know how Damian always says we have a destiny?"

"Yeah." In fact, ever since Nick had arrived to live with his newfound family, at least once a day, Damian or Theo reminded him of his destiny: magic, caviar, and borscht.

"We also have a legacy."

They set the little mice down on the hay. The tiny family now huddled together and looked up at Isabella. Occasionally, Pasha patted her with his delicate paw, as if offering her comfort.

"A legacy? What? Like an inheritance or something?"

"Sort of. Nick, you know how you can Gaze?"

He thought of how his crystal ball was cold earlier, but he nodded. "Yeah."

"In some families, you inherit being a good athlete. Or being a talented singer. In ours, you inherit your magic gifts. When a baby is born in the clan, everyone watches for a sign of what gifts the baby has inherited. When I was born, everyone hoped that I would inherit the gifts of animal magic like my older sister, but no one knew for sure. Some only inherit minor magic."

Nick nodded. The Winter Palace Casino and Hotel had one of the world's most famous orchestras. The players were flawless musicians—critics said that they were equal to the New York Philharmonic and other famous symphony orchestras, but in some ways, they were more amazing, because all of the players were family. There were no auditions. None of them had ever been to music school or conservatory. While brilliant musicians, to the clan, the gift of music, as they called it, was a "minor" magical skill. Animal magic, Gazing, swordplay, spells, levitation—these were parts of the major arts.

Isabella gathered her knees close against her body, tucking her chin down. "The family watched me, but for a while, I showed no signs of my gift. My father even brought a spider monkey to live with us—one he acquired from Sergei—to see if that might help me. Apparently, the monkey used to make me laugh when I was in my high chair, but I never seemed to communicate with it. And then one day, I was playing with my doll near the tigers—and I heard Sascha speak to me. She was a cub, and I heard her ask me if I wanted to play. I had the gift." She looked at Nick and beamed. "I was so excited."

Nick wished he had Isabella's gift. When he'd first met Isabella, he'd been jealous of her pet tiger. Since then, he had seen Irina and Isabella control lions, polar bears, tigers, an elephant, jaguars—the fiercest animals in the world were like gentle pets. But only girls inherited the animal arts.

"After that, Sascha and I slept in the same room. I played with her, ate with her. We did everything together. We grew up together! Then one day, Sascha and I were playing hide and seek. We were out by the animals when a woman appeared—just like today. She was dressed like a бáбушка, a *babushka*."

"A what?"

"An old woman. A peasant woman. A grandmother. But when I looked at her face, I could see she that was not that old. Then she revealed her true self, and it was Maria, the woman here today with the Shadowkeeper."

"Who is she?"

"She is Rasputin's daughter."

Nick's throat went dry. "What?" he managed to squeak.

Isabella nodded. "Yes. She is a leader of the Shadowkeepers in her own right. She was once a tiger tamer. She has the animal gift, Nick, but she uses it for evil ends. You saw that beast."

Nick thought about the Shadowkeeper. And the ravens. And especially the wolf-like creature. It had pointed ears and a long snout—and sharp-looking teeth. Maria had growled to communicate with it, as if she were a beast, too.

"I guess I hadn't really thought that Shadows could use the animal arts."

Isabella tucked a stray hair behind her ear. "Theo says that all magic can be used for light or used for dark. They are two sides to the same coin."

"That creature looked ready to rip us into pieces. And she was just as scary herself."

"She's even scarier than you think, Nick. She tried to take my essence for that vial around her neck! She collects essence."

"Essence? What do you mean?"

"It's a spark. Irina told me that when a Magickeeper is born, a shining star glows deep down inside the child. Part of its flicker is the gift the child inherits, and part is a Magickeeper birthright. Have you not noticed that Magickeepers seem to age differently than humans?"

Nick nodded. "Yeah. Damian and Theo, they look much younger than they are. And the Grand Duchess—she's *really* old, but she's still alive."

"It's the magic part of us. I have it. You have it. But a child's essence is very powerful, Nick. It's innocent. It's the closest people are in their lifetime to the purity of who they are supposed to be."

Nick though of all the jars of potions and ingredients in Theo's classroom. "Does Theo have any child essence in a vial?"

"Of course not! Theo and Damian are honorable. They know better than to mess with the dark arts. But Maria cast a spell on me. Hold my hand."

Nick reached out and took his cousin's hand. In a flash, he was inside her mind as she relived the spell. He felt a suffocating closeness, the stench of a Shadowkeeper. Isabella fell to the ground—hard. Her head smashed against the paved stones. Above her stood Maria, hissing. Nick felt a terrible pain rushing through him, almost as if his entire body were on fire and poison coursed through his veins. Unable to bear the agony, he released his cousin's hand. "You must have been terrified. You were just a little girl!"

She nodded as a single tear fell on to her knee. "I don't even remember what happened after that—the last thing I could recall was her standing over me, licking her hideous red lips. But Sascha attacked her—and then the commotion and Sascha's roars brought Irina and Damian."

"What happened after that?"

"Maria disappeared. And I was very sick for a long time. It

was worse than having the flu. All I wanted to do was sleep and sleep and sleep. Weeks went by—but eventually, with Theo's potions, I was brought back to health. When I was a little older, I found out that Maria had stolen the essence of another Magickeeper—my great-grandmother, who was gifted in the animal arts. Her tiger died trying to protect her, but it was too late."

Nick shuddered. In his mind, he saw a tiger fighting a Shadowkeeper, its fur being shredded by the long, evil talons.

"So their power is stronger than a tiger. Stronger than a polar bear," he said, remembering the time the bears had protected him, their white fur crimson from the blood of their wounds.

"Yes, Nick."

"But what would Maria *do* with your essence if she got it?"

"A captured soul, captured essence, increases their power—and their thirst for blood and all things dark. It helps them live longer, and it can heal them."

"I'm so glad she didn't get you, Isabella."

"Me, too. But that is our legacy. Us against them. Going back through time."

He bit his lip. "This isn't good, Isabella. Why did Maria come here tonight? To try again?"

She shrugged. "I don't know. We have to tell Irina."

"Tell me what?"

Nick and Isabella spun and saw Irina standing behind them, dressed in her usual black riding pants, Russian folk shirt, and vest in a rich, green color that matched her eyes. Sascha crouched by her side.

Nick stood and held out a hand to Isabella to help her up. They brushed hay off their clothes.

"Maria was here," Isabella whispered. "We came to the stalls because…" She glanced at Nick.

"Because we wanted to visit Maslow," Nick blurted. He didn't want Irina to know that they had come to protect the mice alone. She would be upset that they hadn't brought more protection. Of course, now he wished that they had.

Irina blinked slowly, and she pressed her lips together into a straight and very serious line. "Maria? You two come along. We'll have to tell Damian."

Nick and Isabella scooped up the mice and left the stall. Out in the courtyard, Irina approached the biggest tiger—his name was Arkady. She leaned over and spoke seriously, in a hushed yet urgent voice, to the tiger in Russian, her voice rising and falling, sounding very angry at times.

"What is she saying?" Nick asked.

"I can't hear her," Isabella said.

When Irina was done, she turned and led Nick and Isabella back toward the hotel.

"What did you say to Arkady?" Isabella asked.

Irina stopped, turned slowly, and looked at them. "I told him that if Maria dares to appear in the animal area again, he is not to show her any mercy. Her arrival within days of the convention can only mean one thing: the Shadowkeepers are near."

She turned around and strode ahead of them so quickly that they had to run to catch up with her. When they got to the family floors of the hotel, Damian came running from his library, his long hair flying behind him.

"Irina! Kolya! Isabella!" He ran toward them. "Have you heard?"

Irina nodded. "Yes. Maria was here."

Damian's face darkened. "No…that cannot be."

"We saw her," Isabella said solemnly. "Out by the animals. She had a Shadowkeeper with her."

"This is worse than I feared."

"What were *you* going to tell us?" Nick asked cautiously.

"Shadowkeepers have been spotted in nearly every city as the convention draws near. We are certain they are preparing to attack."

"So what do we do?" Nick asked.

"We also prepare, cousin. We prepare."

THE UNITED NATIONS OF MAGIC

HE FIRST DAY OF THE CONVENTION, NICK AND ISABELLA
went down to the lobby of the hotel. Something was
wrong. Usually, the hotel was what guests called "breathtaking."
Nick remembered the first time he stepped into the perfect
re-creation of the majesty of the Tsars and their palaces. Marble
floors and columns had delicate veining through their stone in
a variety of colors from creamy white to pale pink to rich green.
Brocades covered the couches and chairs throughout the lobby,
and the dark-wood furniture was edged with bright gilding. The
center of the lobby was a perfect replica of the semicircular hall
of the Tsar. Its sweeping domes and windows rose opulently,
with ornate alabaster carvings at the top of marble columns.

But on the first day of the convention, their grand and
wonderful hotel was a mess.

Nick surveyed the lobby and scratched his head. Damian was literally flying near the ceiling, circling the lobby until he was no more than a whir. Scaffolding covered the enormous interior one end to the other, scaling the walls. Paint tarps covered furniture. Family members wore the coveralls of construction workers and painters. The place was a disaster.

Isabella sat down on the grand staircase to watch. "What's going on?"

"I don't know, but I'm going to go find out," Nick said. He walked over to the sightseeing desk to visit his dad and grandfather. His father was dressed in the familiar Winter Palace uniform—the men wore the uniforms of the Imperial bodyguards from the early 1900s, complete with gold braiding and Romanov eagles. Nick's father looked very proud in his uniform, with his sandy blond hair combed neatly and his gray eyes peering out from beneath his cap. Grandpa, on the other hand, couldn't even close his uniform jacket over his large belly.

Dad used to be a terrible stage magician, back when they had lived at the Pendragon. He was human, but Nick's mother had been a Magickeeper. His dad had hoped that he could raise Nick anonymously, far from the clan, far from the Shadowkeepers. It was what his mother had wanted.

But when the Shadowkeepers came after Nick, his dad had agreed with his grandfather—his mom's father—to let Nick be raised with the family in the Winter Palace. He knew that only the Magickeepers could keep him safe. He thought it would be temporary.

But when the Shadowkeepers had nearly killed Nick, Damian thought it best if his grandpa and father came to live at the hotel, too. Since they were not Magickeepers, they could not live on the top three floors, but they shared a luxurious apartment on the first floor—the nicest place his father had ever lived! And after years of bickering, the two men had learned to be roommates—and now ran a sightseeing business together out of the lobby.

Nick gestured at the scaffolding and then at his high-flying cousin. "What the *heck* is going on?"

"The Winter Palace is closed," Nick's dad said.

"What do you mean, we're closed?"

His grandfather laughed, and his handlebar mustache wriggled. "We are. What? Was something *important* supposed to be happening?"

Nick stared up at the scaffolding. "The convention. People will be arriving soon." Had everyone gone crazy—including Damian? While he certainly didn't feel ready to make Penelope disappear, he had been looking forward to meeting other kids from other countries—Magickeepers from all over the world. But they could hardly have a convention with the hotel in a state of disaster.

"Oh…that," Grandpa said. He started laughing again.

"Dad," Nick pleaded. "What's happening?"

"If people pull up to the Winter Palace Hotel and Casino, they will see large signs saying, 'Closed for renovations.' Only Magickeepers will be allowed in. We don't need to let the rest of the world know what's going on here."

Nick knew that Magickeepers never revealed their magic to the outside world. They avoided letting their spells be seen by humans at all costs—unless it was in such a way, like in the casino's show, that the humans thought it was illusion, sleight of hand, or outright trickery.

"Okay, that explains all the fake construction. But what's Damian doing?"

"Casting a Spell of Mother Tongue," said Grandpa.

"A what?"

"Ever seen the translators at the United Nations?" asked Grandpa.

"No."

"Well, suffice it to say that when you gather clans from Egypt, Nigeria, France, Japan, England, Australia, Sweden, Germany, Greece and more, all in one convention, it's like a gathering of the United Nations of Magicians. How would we understand each other? Not everyone speaks the same language."

"Half the time," Nick muttered, "I don't even understand Damian. And I live here." He'd spent many of his school hours with Theo learning Russian—including the Cyrillic alphabet—but he still hadn't even memorized the letters.

"Precisely," said Grandpa. "The Spell of Mother Tongue allows everyone to speak their own language—the speech becomes translated in the air so you hear it in your own tongue."

"So I'll be able to talk to kids from, say, Japan—and know what they're saying? And they'll know what I'm saying?"

"Exactly, Kolya," his dad said.

"Dad." Nick lowered his voice. He glanced at the ceiling where Damian was still buzzing by in circles, casting his spell. "Please be careful this week. There was a Shadowkeeper here. In the stall. Out by Maslow."

His father's face paled. "Does Damian know?"

"Now he does."

"Nick...you must also be very careful. I nearly lost you once. I couldn't bear the thought of something happening to you."

"I'll be fine."

"Look, son, I know you want to prove yourself as a Magickeeper. I know you want to show the family that you belong here, that you will be as great someday as your cousins. But you are still learning—still training. Damian and Theo have been working at their skills their entire lives. You can't do what they do yet."

"I promise I'll be fine. It's you I worry about." Nick didn't want to point out the obvious. He had magic—even if he was learning, he had it deep down inside. His father did not-unless Nick wanted to count his dad pulling a rabbit out of a hat or the old pull-a-quarter-from-behind-the-ear trick. And his dad wasn't even very good at those.

"Your grandfather and I will be very busy this week. We will be taking some of the convention-goers on a trip to the Hoover Dam. You should come. You…"

His father didn't have to complete the thought. Nick knew what he had been about to say: *You might be safer there than here.*

"Nah." Nick had never been to the Hoover Dam anyway. He wasn't sure what Damian would think of the trip. Damian did not allow Nick or Isabella to leave the hotel grounds. Then again, sometimes what Damian didn't know wouldn't hurt him…

Sometimes, but probably not this time.

☆   ☆   ☆

Nick and Isabella watched the Magickeepers checking into the hotel. Every few minutes, it seemed, cars arrived, and out poured people from all over the world. Or they simply materialized from nowhere.

The clan from Nigeria was very tall, with high cheekbones and almond-shaped, dark eyes. They wore brightly colored scarves wrapped intricately around their heads. The men carried long, carved staffs. Nick looked closely and realized that the carvings were of animals—and that the animals blinked and moved. One snake slithered up and down, up and down, coiling itself around the cane. The clan's rattan suitcases bulged with mysteries Nick was excited to learn about.

Next to arrive was a Parisian clan; their leader, a woman named Madame Pepper, had a shock of white hair and a pet alligator on a leash. Nick had seen her in a scrapbook that Theo had of a trip to Paris when he was younger.

"Do you want to tell me what she is going to do with an alligator?" Nick whispered to Isabella from their vantage point sitting on the grand staircase. They were peering through the banisters like two children on Christmas Eve trying to peek at their presents.

"All I know is it better not try to eat me," she said with a shrug. The alligator looked at them and licked it lips. Sascha instinctively moved closer to Isabella and nudged her.

The Greek magicians arrived with their own band playing folk music and dancing. Apparently, the Greek Magickeepers liked to break plates—all of them—for fun, so Damian had switched the Winter Palace plates with more casual plates in the dining room.

The Australians had kangaroos. The British contingency was very loud and dressed as a soccer team on holiday for a disguise. They even kicked a soccer ball around—albeit a magical soccer ball that floated up forty feet to the ceiling in the lobby before bouncing back down again and ricocheting across every wall.

"I want to play with *them*," Nick said, laughing.

Commotion and noise filled the air, but even though people spoke their native tongues, Damian's spell allowed them all to communicate.

As the Magickeepers continued to arrive, filling the lobby with bands, animals, people, and large and odd-shaped boxes and suitcases, Nick scanned the crowds for anyone suspicious—anyone who looked like Maria, or like Rasputin.

"Isabella…" He grabbed his cousin's hand. "There!"

A woman stood at the back of a line waiting to check in. Tall and thin, her face was turned the other way. She was dressed in a long black dress that swept the floor—but her immense headdress was what caught Nick's eye. Her broad-brimmed black hat looked three feet wide and was covered in shining black feathers. At the crown of the hat was a stuffed bird.

"She's wearing a raven." Nick elbowed Isabella. "Look at her."

As if she'd heard them from across the lobby, the woman whirled around, fixing her black-eyed stare on Nick. Her face was young—beautiful even, with high cheekbones, a regal nose, and porcelain skin—but her eyes looked ancient. And, Nick decided, evil.

"Who is she?" he whispered.

Isabella shrugged. "I don't know, but I don't trust her."

"Maybe she was the one who brought all those ravens into the sky."

Nick and Isabella watched, scarcely breathing. As the woman turned to walk to the elevators, a huge raven flew across the lobby and landed on her shoulder. Amidst all the other guests, with their alligators and kangaroos, and even a camel and a Komodo dragon, the raven didn't attract much attention. But Nick saw it.

More than that, he felt almost a pinch near his heart, and then that invisible black thread drawing him toward the huge black bird. The room spun slightly, and he held on to the banister. He was certain it was the same raven that had been spying on him.

CHAPTER
8

A DANGEROUS THEFT

ICK STOOD IN FRONT OF THE MIRROR IN HIS ROOM, GETTING dressed for dinner. He sighed and stared at his reflection. A tuxedo! The bow tie was choking him. The old joke (which his father never tired of telling) was right: a tuxedo made a guy look like a penguin. Well, it was just for one night. He turned from the mirror as his crystal ball—perched on its gold pedestal, seeming to sulk for the past few days— suddenly filled with inky smoke, and for a minute, Nick was light-headed.

"You're back," he whispered.

He knew it was strange to talk to a crystal ball, but as Theo had taught, the ball was alive to him in many ways—almost a kindred spirit. Nick ran over and pressed his palms flat against its smooth, round surface. The ball warmed beneath his touch.

"Yes!" His Gazing was back. Nick breathed slowly and opened his...well, *soul*—he didn't know how else to describe it. When he Gazed, he felt as if a *whoosh* of air shot up from his stomach and into his thumping heart before leaving him.

In his mind, he flashed on ravens. Hundreds of them. Blackness all around. The birds were flying over him, near him, beating against him with their wings. He felt their feathers brushing his cheeks, their beaks pulling on his clothing. And he heard a deafening roar. It was so loud that he fell to his knees, took his hands from the ball, and covered his ears. But then he realized that the roar was only in his mind.

He didn't even hear Isabella and Sascha come in.

"Nick, what's wrong?" His cousin ran to his side and knelt next to him.

"They're here. I know they are." His breath came in shallow gasps, and he swatted at the empty air, as if beating the ravens away. "Back! Get back!" he yelled at the unseen birds. The roar continued in his mind, driving him crazy. "Can't you hear them? Can't you? Back!"

"Nick! Nick! Snap out of it!" Isabella pinched his arm really hard in the soft place near his armpit.

"*Ow!*" he screamed—but it jolted him out of his vision.

"Look at me."

He looked at his cousin. There she was, kneeling next to her tiger. No ravens. No blackness. No danger. Just Isabella.

Same dark brown hair, same skinny arms, same slightly turned-up nose. Same lopsided smile—only now her mouth was bent into a crooked frown of concern.

"Sorry," he said softly. "It was a vision. I saw…ravens. Like at the stalls. Hundreds of them. Thousands. Attacking me. Their caws were in my ears. Their sharp beaks were pecking at me."

Sascha nudged him with her slightly damp coal-colored nose, her fur thick as a carpet. The tiger licked his face, her tongue as wide as his forehead, purring loudly. Nick wiped the tiger slobber away. "Stop it, Sascha. I'm fine now."

"We'll just have to keep a very close eye on the woman with the raven," stated Isabella.

"*Spy on her* is more like it." Nick struggled to his feet. "We better go to dinner."

"A tuxedo?" Isabella raised one eyebrow, suppressing a smile.

"Damian insisted." Nick looked his cousin up and down. She was dressed in an eighteenth-century Russian dress the color of emeralds, with lace and finery and intricate embroidery. Jewels were sewn into the high lace collar. Isabella's hair was held up with pins, and two emerald combs were tucked into her chignon. "You look very nice, too, Isabella," he said dryly.

"Irina insisted." She sighed. "Many of the families will be in costumes from their home countries. But I hate the lace. It itches!"

The two of them—and Sascha—rode down in the elevator. Nick tried to put the ravens from his mind and concentrate instead on the fact that they were actually getting to eat in the hotel ballroom instead of on the top floor with the family.

"Do you think we'll be able to have real food?" he asked. "Not borscht? Or fish-egg crepes?" He was envisioning a real, all-you-can-eat Las Vegas buffet like the ones he used to go to with Grandpa. Cheeseburgers. Chicken fingers in little animal shapes—he didn't care if they were dinosaur-shaped or had elephant ears, as long as he could drown them in honey mustard. He pictured French fries, and maybe pizza bagels, and sliced prime rib. And dessert! Pies, cakes, ice cream sundaes, mousse—he wanted chocolate mousse covered with whipped cream. And fizzy orange soda, not bitter Russian tea.

When they arrived in the downstairs ballroom, it was decorated all in white, like a snow-covered Russian castle. White muslin hung from the ceilings, and swirling, delicate snowflakes fell in small flurries here and there. Trees had sprouted from the floor, their roots penetrating the parquet, their branches bare of leaves. The whole place was a vision from a Siberian winter.

"It's beautiful," Isabelle sighed.

They walked to their table, which had an enormous snow globe with a white Siberian tiger inside it as a centerpiece.

"Look!" Isabella grinned. "It looks just like Sascha."

The tiger inside moved and blinked its eyes.

"It is magnificent," said a young boy with bright white teeth, black eyes, and smooth, coffee-colored skin. "So lifelike."

Isabella nodded.

"You must be Nicholai and Isabella," the visitor said.

Now Nick nodded. "Yeah. But you can call me Nick."

"I am Atsu, and this is my twin sister, Siti." He gestured toward a girl with long black hair that fell to her waist. She was fidgeting in a crisp white dress, clearly as uncomfortable as Nick and Isabella were in their formal wear. Both of the twins had green eyes. "We are from Egypt."

Nick and Isabella sat down. Sascha flopped on the shiny wooden floor in back of Isabella's chair.

"I hear you are a Gazer," Atsu said. "My gift is Divination. I can read the stars and tell the future. My sister can touch an object and see its past."

Isabella gestured at Sascha. "Animal arts."

"Oooh," Siti cooed. "I would *so* love to have that gift. I've been begging my papa for a cat—a simple house cat—but he says he is allergic. I would give anything to have a cat like yours. But it is not my destiny."

"You can pet Sascha. She's very sweet." Isabella bent to Sascha and instructed her to go to Siti's chair. Their new friend ran her fingers through Sascha's fur.

"She's magnificent," Siti said. "Her coat...it's so beautiful. I don't think I've ever touched anything so soft in all my life."

Nick nodded. "Sascha is very cool. I wasn't sure we were going to be friends when we first met."

"I had heard you were raised with the outsiders," Siti remarked softly, her eyes still on Sascha. "That you just joined your family this year. What is it like? The outside?"

"I never knew anything different until I came here. I skateboarded. Played video games."

"What are video games?" Atsu asked.

"Well, it's like playing with magic, in a way. You have this controller, and you go through worlds, and..." Nick furrowed his brow. "It's hard to explain. Besides, real magic is a lot cooler. Though outsider food is better." He grinned. "At least American food. Las Vegas-style."

"Maybe someday I will try it!" Atsu exclaimed.

"So what's Egypt like? I've always wanted to go there. Have you seen the pyramids?"

"I have. Siti has, too, but she doesn't ever go there anymore. My sister—it's too painful for her."

"When I touch the walls of the pyramids," Siti said, "I can feel the horrific lives of the slaves that built them. Their sacrifices remain in the energy of the stone. So many people lost in death through suffering. So I no longer visit."

Before Nick could reply, there was a *tink-tink-tink-tink* sound.

Damian stood at the head banquet table and tapped an ornate, sterling silver spoon against his crystal water glass. Soon, others picked up their glasses.

Tink-tink-tink-tink. Tink-tink-tink-tink.

The chatter in the ballroom ceased, and everyone gazed expectantly at Nick's older cousin. Nick, as always, marveled at the way he stood: confident and completely in control. Damian never felt a bit nervous performing in front of thousands of people—or standing in front of all these magicians. Even Nick had to admit it: Damian was a leader.

"Welcome, Magickeepers from around the world. Welcome! It is a joy and an honor to have you all gathered in our humble little hotel for our convention."

At the word *humble*, people in the crowd chuckled.

Damian surveyed the room. "We are an example for all of humankind, gathered peacefully to learn from each other, honor each other, and share in our united history tracing back to ancient Egypt. These are dangerous times," he continued, his face darkening. "Shadowkeepers would gladly disrupt us, steal our artifacts, and try to bring harm to us. But are we afraid?"

The crowd murmured, "No," in unison.

"Our history has been one of persecution, of immense danger, yet we have never strayed from what we know is right. Magic can be a force for good. Or it can be a force for evil. Our choice, my dear friends, is to stand by and allow the Shadowkeepers to grow in strength and power, or to boldly fight them where they strike."

Across the large hall, Magickeepers clapped. Nick felt an excited surge run up his spine. Yes, his older cousin could be arrogant and difficult, but he was also inspiring.

"Our choice was always and remains…to be united. To lift each other up. To live in solidarity. I tell you, my fellow Magickeepers, we shall live our lives by the words of that great and illustrious Magickeeper, Sir Isaac Newton." Damian raised his glass in a toast. *"If I have seen further than others, it is by standing on the shoulders of giants. To magic!"*

"To magic!" repeated the crowd.

"And now, tonight, we host you Russian-style." Damian clapped his hands, and silver trays floated into the dining room with bowls full of the red beet soup Nick loathed.

A bowl placed itself in front of Nick. He stared down into its deep red ickiness. "I was hoping for pizza," he said to Isabella.

She laughed. "Perhaps we can play Magic Eights with Siti and Atsu later and order some from Sergei."

"Done and done." He lifted his spoon as strolling *bandura* players plucked their instruments, playing folk songs of courage and Mother Russia. Nick often wished he'd been blessed with the gift of song; the voices of the *bandura* players were haunting, and he felt his throat tighten. Yet he couldn't help but wonder why they were not allowed to sing modern songs. He knew he'd never see *Kalinka* on MTV.

"This is it," Nick heard himself say. "There is no escaping my destiny."

Isabella scowled at him, but Nick grinned at her. "It's okay, Isabella. I'm used to it by now."

As the evening wore on, other clans brought out their folk instruments. The Tibetans performed *nang ma* with a *dramnyen*, which looked like a lute; a *pe wang*, which was very much like a fiddle; and *gling,* which were bells that sounded light and happy. Nick could almost imagine them being played high in the Himalayas.

The Greek clan performed next. (They'd only stopped for Damian's toast.) Nick noticed how the Caledonian costumes—white blouses underneath black vests, with red embroidered skirts on the women and black pants on the men—were a *lot* like the Russian folk costumes. Maybe Damian was right. Maybe all the world was actually more alike than different. The Greeks played *tabachaniotika* songs on their *bouzoukis*. Soon, everyone was dancing. Some Magickeepers climbed on tables; some danced on the parquet floor with its intricate diamond pattern; some simply flew up from their chairs, levitating and twirling in the air.

"*Hopa!*" someone shouted.

A plate was dropped from one of the Greeks dancing near the ceiling. It smashed on the dance floor.

"*Hopa!*" others called out.

Plates smashed. Then one of the Greeks cast a reversal spell—the plates pieced themselves together again and flew back up, only to be smashed once more.

Nick grinned at Siti and Atsu. "Come on!" They grabbed their plates, climbed on top of the table, and smashed the plates to the floor in the style of Greek celebration.

Nick surveyed the room. Everyone was smiling or singing or dancing—or flying. He couldn't remember ever having so much fun or feeling so happy in his entire life. For the first time since he knew Shadowkeepers existed and wanted to harm him, he was free among Magickeepers. He felt safe and warm and filled with something he had never quite felt before. He belonged.

Then suddenly there was a shout from the far corner of the room.

"*Stop! Stop!* Please! Help!"

"It is my father!" Siti exclaimed, grabbing Nick's arm, her black eyes widening in alarm.

The Greek band stopped playing mid-note. Magickeepers descended from the ceiling like deflating balloons. Others climbed down from tables and returned to their seats. A frightened hush fell over the ballroom.

"What is it, Jahi?" Damian asked.

"A most terrible thing has happened!"

"Tell us," Theo said.

"The Pyramid of Souls has been stolen."

THE GREAT PYRAMID

W HAT IS THE PYRAMID OF SOULS?" NICK ASKED ATSU.
The entire room was now whispering; the sound
was like buzzing bees in the cavernous ballroom. The adults
huddled in corners, their voices echoing and ricocheting off
the walls. Nick saw Theo and Damian fly—literally—from
the ballroom.

"The Pyramid of Souls is a soul house," said his new friend.

"What's that?"

"They are from way back in history—centuries and centuries ago. The great pharaohs' tombs were marked with clay
soul houses. People believed souls could be collected in them.
It was a bit of superstition. They were just clay. But some of
the Egyptian Magickeepers had a real soul house."

"What do you mean...*real?*"

"It could collect souls—essences—and store them for safe-keeping. The soul house was forged of gold and encrusted with jewels, and then a spell was cast over it by one of the first Magickeepers of Egypt. The intention, of course, was to fight Shadowkeepers. To collect evil souls and lock them away where they could do no harm. But in the wrong hands? It is too powerful a relic. Somehow, though, it was stolen by grave robbers centuries ago. Our family spent those centuries trying to reclaim the Pyramid of Souls. It changed hands many times—a very complicated history. But finally, we regained it. We have been the guardians of the Pyramid of Souls for three generations now."

Nick thought of Damian's vault. In the deepest basement of the Winter Palace Hotel and Casino was a vault of money: the one the family showed to the gaming commission, which oversaw all the casinos. But hidden there was another vault—one that housed all of the family's relics and artifacts, the magic that they guarded and kept safe. The Eternal Hourglass that he, Theo, and Damian had recaptured rested there, inside a glass case.

"You brought the Pyramid of Souls here? To the convention?"

Atsu nodded. "We always travel with it. The pyramid is too important to leave behind. This news is very dangerous. In the hands of Shadowkeepers, the pyramid could collect the souls of those in Sanctuary."

"What's that?" Nick asked.

"It is a place where Magickeepers go when they disappear—a resting place. It is also a place where Magickeepers are vulnerable—a place where the soul house easily could be used to capture their essences."

Nick looked at Isabella and lowered his voice. "What if the raven lady took it?"

Isabella nodded. "We should never have let her out of our sight. Do you see her in the ballroom?"

Nick scanned the crowd. He spotted her—looking over her shoulder and scurrying from the room. While everyone else was fretting over the theft, she was *leaving*.

"There, Isabella!" he hissed. "She's up to something."

"What are you two whispering about?" Siti asked. "Do you know who has our clan's soul house? You have no idea what the Pyramid of Souls can do." Siti's eyes were wide with terror. "We are its guardians. If we have lost it, no one is safe."

Nick exchanged a look with Isabella. "Come on. Let's go. You two can come. We'll explain as we go."

With all the adults in an uproar, the four of them slipped out of the ballroom with Sascha on their heels. Out in the lobby, Nick looked for the raven woman, but she was nowhere to be seen. *What did I expect?* he thought. A Shadowkeeper could disappear with the snap of a finger and the blink of an eye.

"We need to find out what's going on," said Nick. "Let's

start in the classroom. Maybe one of Theo's crystal balls will tell us what we need to know."

✿ ✿ ✿

The four of them—and Sascha—snuck into the empty classroom. Nick heard the skittering sounds of bugs and spiders in their glass jars, the chirping of crickets, and some *gloops* and *pops* and *hisses*—he wasn't sure he wanted to know where those sounds came from. Nick squinted and looked at the rows of crystal balls—some glowed in the darkness—but he was too afraid to turn on a light and attract attention.

"If you were going to try to find out something about an ancient Egyptian artifact, which ball would you choose?" he asked Atsu.

The tall, dark-haired boy walked to the crystal balls and surveyed them, one by one, until he came to a ball that stood atop a gold pedestal. Each of the feet on the pedestal was shaped like a sphinx, and hieroglyphics were etched in the base.

"This one!" He pointed. "Don't you agree, Siti?"

His sister nodded solemnly. "Yes, Atsu. That is a wise choice."

Nick stared at the ball. He was in big trouble if Theo caught him. His cousin didn't like anyone Gazing in his collection without permission, just as Damian didn't allow anyone in his library. But trouble or not, this was an emergency, and everyone was panicked and frenzied with worry downstairs. Who would look for them there? He touched the ball and waited for a vision in his mind.

The first time he had ever Gazed, Madame B. and Grandpa had told him never to make assumptions. But now, staring into a ball on a sphinx pedestal, he expected to see Egypt. Instead, he had a vision of a disheveled, nineteenth-century American writer...

☆ ☆ ☆

Ryan's Saloon, Lombard Street, Baltimore, Maryland, September 28, 1849

Edgar Allan Poe was passed out on a wooden bench outside a noisy saloon when a passerby poked him. "You there, drunkard! Move along!"

Poe sat up, his face clearly panicked and terrified. He stared down at his clothes. "These clothes! These are not mine!"

His attire was tattered and cheap. Seams were ripped, threads dangled loosely about, the elbows and knees were worn, and the suit itself did not fit him properly. It was far too big for his shoulders and hung on him like the suit for a farmer's scarecrow. He wore a brimless hat, crushed and unkempt, with unsightly moth holes. He himself was dirty and unwashed. He patted himself as if searching for a pocket. "The key!" he shouted incoherently, his eyes wide but unseeing.

"What say you, man? What say you?"

"The key!"

"I shall fetch a constable." The passerby went to search for a policeman.

Poe shook his head as if to shake off his slumber. His eyes registered fear. He tugged at his face, at his tumble of black hair, a haunted expression on his face.

"I promise you, I do not have it," he said to no one, to the Baltimore air. A stiff wind blew his hat away, and it tumbled down the sidewalk.

Then, across the dark gray sky, ravens flew, gathering on rooftops like black sentinels, peering down at Poe solemnly.

"They are here!" one cawed. "They are here!"

A chorus of cawing birds shrieked.

Down the street in the dirty gutter, littered with newspaper, a black ooze slithered, oily and rich, dark and evil.

"No!" cried Poe. "No! No! *Help!*" he shrieked wildly, cowering. "*Help!*"

The passerby reappeared around the corner, accompanied by a constable.

"See!" said the man. "Incoherent. A drunkard, no doubt!"

The constable—blue uniform pressed, brass buttons

shining—approached the bench, his hand on his nightstick. Poe shrunk back in fear.

"I tell you, I do not have it!" said Poe. "I do not have it!"

Then the famed writer shuddered, eyes rolling back in his head. He collapsed on the bench, unconscious, as the ravens took to the sky and flew toward the crescent moon.

A JOURNEY TO THE DESERT

"So what does that mean?" Siti asked Nick.

The four of them peered into the ball as the last vision of Edgar Allan Poe faded away and the crystal grew cold.

"I don't know." Nick furrowed his brow. "I don't get it. What does that show us about the relic? Maybe I got my Gazing wires crossed or something."

Suddenly, Sergei's face filled the crystal ball. "*Nick!* My friend, my pal, my sixth cousin twice removed…"

"Sergei!" Nick snapped. "Not now. This is urgent. We're looking for something."

"Then have I got just the thing for you: a bloodhound."

"A bloodhound?"

"Yes, this very dog was owned by Queen Victoria! He can sniff out anything." Behind Sergei, Nick could see a brown dog with floppy jowls and sad, rheumy eyes resting its head on its large paws.

"If Queen Victoria owned that dog, then it's ancient. In dog years, it must be like a thousand years old. Forget it, Sergei."

"All right, all right. Then I have something else for you. Something extraordinary!"

"What?" Nick looked in the ball sternly.

"An African rat. It's a sniffer rat."

"You're making that up," said Isabella. "There's no such thing."

Siti leaned over to Isabella and whispered, "Who is this strange little man?"

"Strange little man?" Sergei shouted. "I am the greatest black-market dealer the magical world has ever known! You need a chattering monkey? You call me. You need a dancing bear that can count to ten? You call me. You need a llama that can tap dance to the balalaika, you just speak into the ball! You need pizza and Chinese food at two in the morning? You call me! The name's Crazy Sergei. My prices are INSANE!"

Atsu laughed. "I think every family has someone like Sergei. In our family, his name is Chisisi."

Sergei chuckled. "I know Chisisi. He once cheated me in cards."

"That doesn't surprise me," Atsu replied.

"Come on. You want the African sniffer rat or not? I give you good deal, Kolya."

"What is a sniffer rat?" Nick asked.

"Trained to sniff anything. Like a bloodhound. I trained him with cheese balls. The sniffer rat is the real deal. Come on, Kolya. We're old pals. You and your family know me."

"Indeed, we do," came Theo's voice from behind them. "No rats!"

Nick whirled around. "Theo, I can explain."

"You can explain how it is you came to be in my classroom, peering into crystal balls that belong to *me*? Negotiating for a rodent with Sergei? You can explain?" Theo towered over them, scowling.

"We were trying to help."

"Help do what?"

"Recover the Pyramid of Souls," Nick said, swallowing. "We thought if we looked in the right crystal ball, we could find out who took it." He hesitated, already positive the raven lady stole it. "And then we could help get it back."

"And you thought this ball, with the sphinxes, would tell you where it was," Theo finished for him.

Nick nodded.

"Do you really know how dangerous the loss of the Pyramid of Souls is?" Theo demanded, straightening his long robes.

Nick looked at Isabella, and then at the twins. All four of them slowly shook their heads. "I mean, I know it's not good," Nick said.

"Come along. All four of you! Sascha, my friend, you must remain." Theo snapped his fingers. It took no longer than a blink: Nick felt himself hurtling, and when he exhaled—and opened his eyes—he, Isabella, and the twins were standing next to Theo in a blazing hot desert.

Camels clopped along, bending their funny knobby knees. There was sand beneath their feet, and the sky was cloudless and a pinkish-gray hue.

Nick shielded his eyes. "Where are we?"

"Sanctuary."

Nick loosened the bow tie on his tuxedo. "It's so hot!"

"Come," Theo said. "We will remedy that."

In front of Nick, a huge pyramid rose up from the shifting sands. As they walked closer, the shadow it cast made the air a tiny bit cooler. The stones were tremendous, each one the size of a small room.

Nick and Isabella followed Theo as he walked to a small doorway and stepped inside the pyramid. Atsu and Siti stood outside.

"My sister feels it is best if she does not enter," said Atsu.

Nick nodded. "I understand."

Siti looked at him solemnly, her dark eyes filled with

sadness. "The true Great Pyramids were constructed from pain. Even if Sanctuary was constructed magically, there is too much history in her walls. I cannot touch the stones."

"I will wait here with her," Atsu said.

"See you soon, then," Nick said.

The temperature dropped even more after a step or two inside the pyramid, and Nick blinked a few times as his eyes adjusted to the dimness after the bright sun. He touched the stone walls. Hieroglyphics were carved deep into the rock. His fingers slid into the recesses of stone. The figures seemed to quiver in front of his eyes. He assumed it was his eyes adjusting to the interior of the pyramid after the brilliant light outside. Then Nick poked Isabella. "Look!"

Sure enough, the figures moved. This wasn't just any pyramid—that would be amazing enough. Nick could feel magic all around them. Along the walls, as Nick and Isabella walked, flames from lanterns lit the way, casting the stone in an eerie orange glow. The hieroglyphic figures followed them on either side of the hall. They had a peculiar way of walking—their hands jutting out at right angles, their necks thrust forward. They walked rhythmically and in uniform fashion, like trained soldiers. Some of the figures had depictions of dogs, wolves, or birds with long legs beside them.

"What is this place?" Nick whispered to Isabella.

"It's part of Newton's Fourth Law," she said. "If you disappear in the real world, you must then equally appear in the mirror on the other side, the magical realm. You can't simply disappear into nothingness. We may be magical, but we are flesh and blood, too. We are matter. This space has been declared a Sanctuary."

The passageway narrowed. Theo turned sideways, and so did Nick and Isabella. Now Nick heard murmured voices—and music. When they reached the end of the passage, they emerged in a cavernous room. A banquet table ran along one stone wall, laden with roasts and fancy dishes; at one end were cakes and pies and puddings set on silver platters.

"This is like one of the all-you-can-eat buffets Grandpa takes me to," said Nick, smiling in spite of his nervousness. "Now *this* is food I could dig in to." He looked at the platters and tureens. "And no borscht!" His mouth watered.

All around, people in every kind of costume imaginable stood chatting. A string quartet played a whimsical waltz. Two men sat at one table, wearing tuxedos and playing a game of chess, only the pieces—complete with small horses for knights—were magical and moved themselves.

"Who *are* all these people?" Nick whispered to Theo.

"They are magicians. All of them are here, disappeared from the real world, for a time. It could be as part of an act. It could be because they are hiding."

Nick spied a large lion with a magnificent golden mane sitting in the corner, gnawing on a juicy steak. "I guess someone made a lion disappear."

"Exactly. So when you make Penelope and Isabella disappear, this is where they will come. And when you retrieve them, this is where you will get them."

"Why do you call it Sanctuary?" Nick asked.

Theo lowered his voice. "See that man over there?"

Nick and Isabella looked in the direction he gestured. The man was dressed in a black suit and was playing a game of solitaire with quietly chattering cards.

"Yes," Isabella whispered.

"That man is D. B. Cooper."

"Who's that?" Isabella asked.

"He's a Magickeeper—and an outlaw. He jumped out of a plane with $200,000 and was never seen or heard from again."

Nick stared at the man. "How long has he been missing?"

"Over thirty years."

"Has he been here all that time?"

"No. It is not wise to stay in Sanctuary for a long time. But the fact is, the Magickeepers are furious with him. He called attention to us—unwanted attention. Sure, he tried to cover it up by parachuting, but then he disappeared...and for what reason? For a mere $200,000? It was for the thrill. But"—Theo lowered his voice even more—"in Sanctuary, all are respected. No fights may occur here. It's a neutral zone. So even though D. B. Cooper angered the Magickeepers, here…nothing is said."

"Though no one is playing cards with him," Isabella noticed.

"That's because he is a sore loser," whispered Theo.

"Can Shadowkeepers come here?" Nick asked.

"No. This is hallowed ground. They would not be comfortable here for long. But out in the desert, I believe they could strike."

Nick watched as a woman in a dazzling magician's assistant costume—all sequins and feathers and glitter—said good-bye to the people nearest her and promptly disappeared.

"So," said Theo, "now that you know where things go when they disappear, it should be easier for you to make Penelope disappear."

"What about the Pyramid of Souls?"

"The pyramids have great meaning to Magickeepers. We are all descended from the original Magickeepers of ancient Egypt. If the Pyramid of Souls was brought here, to hallowed ground and someone collected souls from here, it would—be deadly. No one would expect an assault in Sanctuary. No defensive arts. No battleground here. We must find that relic."

"So who do you think took the Pyramid of Souls, Theo?"

"The Shadowkeepers. But surely they don't want just any soul. They are hoping to capture an important soul." Theo stared down at Nick meaningfully.

Nick bit the inside of his cheek. He didn't like the sound of that. Rasputin, the evil leader of the Shadowkeepers, seemed very intent on having Nick join him. And if Nick wouldn't join him...then Rasputin wanted to destroy him. Nick just didn't know why he was so important.

The three made their way back through the narrow staircase and out into the desert. Collecting Siti and Atsu, Theo swept his hand, and again, in the space of time it took Nick to blink, he felt a *whoosh* in the pit of his stomach and found himself standing back in their classroom.

Theo said, "Now, all four of you, off to bed. Let me worry about the Pyramid of Souls. There's been enough excitement for the night."

Nick had no intention of falling asleep. From experience, he knew that when it came to magic—his family's magic—the "excitement" was probably just beginning. And so was the danger. He was determined to make sure, once again, that the Shadowkeepers didn't get what they were after...whatever that was.

ANYTHING BOYS CAN DO,
GIRLS CAN DO, TOO!

*I*N THE MIDDLE OF THE NIGHT, NICK FELT AS IF HE COULDN'T breathe. When he jolted himself awake, and realized he *had* fallen asleep despite himself. Then he realized Sascha's two front paws were leaning on his chest. Isabella was next to her, poking Nick in the arm.

"Haven't you heard of knocking?" Nick grumbled.

"Couldn't chance anyone else hearing us."

"What do you want, Isabella?" He ran his hands through his hair and pushed aside Sascha's paws.

"I need you to teach me to sword fight."

He sat up and frowned at his cousin. "Are you insane?"

"No. You saw Maria. I think she is here for me. And what if she and that raven woman have the Pyramid of Souls? What if she captures me?"

"Isabella, no one is going to let that happen."

"Just the same, I want to be able to fight. I'll show them that I'm not a little girl anymore. That I'm as strong as you—as strong as anyone!"

"Isabella, I don't think that's a good idea. Damian and Theo—they're tightening security. Everyone is looking for the Pyramid of Souls. No one is going to let anything happen to you." He nodded at the tiger. "Sascha would never let anything bad happen to you."

"But don't you see, Nick? Other tigers have died in this battle. I could never let anything happen to Sascha. It's the other way around. She's like my sister. I could never let her defend me to the death."

Nick looked into the tiger's eerie blue eyes. Then he looked into his cousin's eyes. All he saw was determination.

"No," he said, equally determined. "Swords? No, Isabella. They're dangerous. You would have to ask Boris."

"Boris thinks I am a baby. Besides, he scares me."

"He scares everyone. His legs are as thick as tree trunks. He's huge!"

"Precisely, so you need to teach me."

"Look, if Boris found out I was teaching you and not him, it would be my head!"

"If you don't teach me, I'll teach myself!"

Nick sighed. "You are the most stubborn girl I have ever met!"

"I'll take that as a compliment."

Nick climbed from his bed. He checked on Vladimir, who was usually hungry at night. His pudgy little hedgehog tended to munch on vegetables, cooked meats, and fruit. But ever since Isabella had told him that Vlad liked worms, Nick put some extra-tasty (at least, he assumed they were tasty!) mealworms in the hedgehog's cage. He patted his pet on his soft little snout. He was trying to think—trying to buy some time to figure out how to talk Isabella out of her crazy scheme.

"If you're trying to stall, it won't work," his cousin said.

"All right!" he relented. He knew better that to try to out-stubborn his cousin. Together, they left his room and tiptoed down the darkened hallway to Boris's training room, with Sascha right behind them.

"If Boris catches us, he'll make Damian look like a teddy bear," Nick whispered.

The two of them gently pushed open the door and stepped into the room, which looked a bit like a karate studio, with hardwood floors ready for training. The difference was the array of swords gleaming on the wall. Boris had hundreds: long and pointed, short and dagger-like. Their metals were shining silver and gold. Some were encrusted with gemstones. Most of them had writing on the hilts or blades—ancient ciphers and symbols from languages long forgotten.

All of them were magical.

Nick's own sword was centuries old and forged by a Japanese swordsmith in magic fire. If Nick had a true heart—if he was not fighting for revenge or for evil—his sword was infallible. It always found its mark and could never slice Nick's own skin. Were he not true of heart…Boris had always told him the results would be bloody.

Sascha entered and sniffed at the floor and walls, pacing.

"Okay," Nick said, "Boris told me your sword picks you, not the other way around."

The words had barely left his mouth when a clanging and clatter arose, and swords flew off the walls. They whistled through the air, moving so fast that all Nick saw were silver and gold streaks slashing through the air. Nick grabbed Isabella's hand as all the swords flew at them, points stopping inches from them until they were literally surrounded by gleaming, deadly blades.

"We can't move," whispered Nick. "It's like they're guarding us."

Either that or imprisoning them, he thought, but he kept that to himself. Isabella was hyperventilating.

Sascha roared and walked around the swords. She even tried to bat one away with her big paw, but it wouldn't budge.

Nick and Isabella stood there for a long time, until Nick's knees ached and his legs started shaking. He tried to command the swords away—but they remained, poised to strike. Sascha paced, clearly agitated.

Finally, when Nick thought he could bear it no longer and his legs would just collapse from having to stand in one spot, Boris walked in.

"Well, what do I have here?" he said, crossing his massive arms across his even more massive chest. The scar on his face—shaped like a starfish, but mostly hidden beneath a black eye patch—reddened angrily.

"We can explain," Isabella squeaked.

"I'm sure you can. In fact, it always seems like you two can *explain* the trouble you get into."

"Honest, Boris," Isabella pleaded, "we promise you we didn't intend—"

"Intend to break in here, and then find yourselves staring at the deadly points of hundreds of swords? Is that it?"

She tried to smile. "Well, when you put it that way…"

"выездной семинар!" Boris shouted.

At his command, the swords all flew back to their places on the wall—all except one.

"This is your sword, Isabella," said Boris gruffly. "Now why don't you tell me what this is all about?"

Isabella glanced at Nick.

He nodded. "Go ahead. He'll find out anyway."

"Boris," she said softly, "we saw Maria in the stalls.

She had a vial around her neck—just like when I was a little girl."

Boris snorted. "You are still a little girl! A tiny little girl who thinks she is a big girl. Ha!"

"Please, Boris. Teach me how to sword fight. I do not want to be captured by Maria."

"You have a tiger."

"But she shouldn't have to die to protect me!"

Boris tapped his finger against his chin. "What should I do with you? What, in the name of all that is Mother Russia, should I do with you?"

"You taught Nick," Isabella pointed out.

"That is different."

"Why?" She crossed her arms over her chest and glared at Boris. "You don't think I can fight?"

Boris walked over to her and looked down—way down, since Boris was easily six feet, six inches tall. "All right, my little impish buttercup, we will see what you are made of."

He wiggled his finger, and the sword, which had been hovering near Isabella, moved to her side. Isabella wrapped her thin fingers around its hilt. It fit her hand perfectly, as if it had been forged precisely for her. The blade was thin—about an inch and a half wide—a blinding, shiny silver without so much as a single scratch. But the best part was that the hilt was carved with the head of a Siberian tiger, with sapphires in its eyes.

Isabella almost dropped the sword. "It's very heavy," she said to Boris.

"Too heavy for such a little buttercup?"

"*No!*" she said stubbornly.

"I will let you in on a little secret." Boris knelt down and looked Isabella in the eyes. "If you seek revenge, if you hold the sword in anger, it will weigh as much as a heavy stone. If you hold it believing that you will use it only to defend your family and your loyal sister, Sascha, it will be as light as a bird's feather and will do you no harm. Do you understand me, little Buttercup?"

Isabella nodded solemnly.

"Now, you think about what is in your heart. You search inside your heart."

"Well, I—"

"Hush," said Boris. "You are like your cousin here." He looked over at Nick. "Always in a hurry to open your mouth with an opinion—very often a *foolish* opinion. No. Think. Take some time and think. In fact, shut your eyes, little Buttercup."

Isabella did as Boris instructed.

"Now breathe. Slowly. And think of your tiger."

Isabella breathed, and Nick watched as the sword, which she could barely lift a moment ago, seemed to rise on its own. Finally, it left her hand and flew around the room.

"Control it with your mind," Boris instructed her, leaning

close and whispering in her ear. "Control your heart. Fill your thoughts with protection. Then control the sword."

He gestured to Nick's sword on the wall. "All right, you shall now practice against each other. Remember, the minute you allow anger into your heart, or impatience, the swords will fail you."

Nick and Isabella faced each other as their swords fought in the air above them. The blades struck each other, sparks flying like Fourth of July sparklers. The clanging was deafening, like marching-band cymbals.

Nick concentrated, moving his sword in his mind with precision, fighting against his cousin's sword. He could not believe that she was such a formidable opponent for her first time fighting him. He broke out in a sweat, every muscle tense with concentration. Though he was not holding the sword, the effort to control it was exhausting. His arms trembled.

"She will start out a *ryadovoy*, a private, and finish a *kapitan*, a captain, at this rate," Boris mused, chuckling slightly to himself.

Finally, the two swords faced each other, point to point.

"I call it a draw!" shouted Boris. The swords dropped to the floor. Boris clapped both Nick and Isabella on the back. "So now I have two sword fighters. Imagine that!"

Isabella—brow sweaty, cheeks flushed with the effort—wiped away a stray hair. "That was fun!"

Boris's face grew stormy again. "Yes, yes, Buttercup. In here, perhaps. But out there...out there with the Shadowkeepers, their swords fight for blood, for death, for evil ends. Never forget that. No fun for you. Not when Maria has been sighted. Not when evil has again decided to come to our home."

"I can't forget about the Shadowkeepers," Isabella said softly. "I can't ever. And even when I want to sometimes, I still have nightmares, and they come to me in my sleep."

"Better to be prepared then..." Boris said. "Let us speak of good now." He spat over his shoulder three times—it was a Russian superstition that if a person said something bad or talked about death, then they had to spit three times and then say something positive instead. When Nick first arrived, he'd felt like all anyone ever did was spit. "We speak of good, so I say to you that you are lucky you have each other. Now both of you—go! And do not let me catch you in here again without permission, or next time, I will leave you all night instead of for just one hour."

"You *knew* we were here?" Nick asked incredulously. "You knew we were standing here, trapped by the swords?"

Boris laughed so loud that his voice echoed off the walls and rattled the swords. "Do you think I would not booby-trap my swords? Especially when Shadowkeepers are lurking in our stalls and stealing the Pyramid of Souls? I am a better soldier and Magickeeper than that."

Nick, Isabella, and Sascha turned to go. They had reached the door when Boris said, "One more thing."

"Yes?" Isabella asked him.

"Do not tell Irina that I trained you in the Cossack sword fighting arts. She will be very angry with me. And an angry Russian woman is worse than even Damian."

THE SECRET OF THE KEYS

*L*ater that night, Nick woke up, certain that Vladimir
was bustling around his cage. Between Isabella and
now Vladimir, he was positive he would be falling asleep at
the breakfast table the next day—which would only infuriate
Damian, since they had rehearsal.

"Quiet, Vlad!" Nick shushed his pet.

But then he realized it wasn't Vladimir at all. It was his crystal
ball. Or, more precisely, it was a large black raven inside the ball.

✧　✧　✧

Richmond, Virginia, September 21, 1849
"Do you understand what I am asking of you, Edgar Allan
Poe?" inquired the raven, her voice lilting and raspy.

The writer was sweating, panic-stricken. His shirt collar stuck to his neck. He mopped his brow. He had sworn off alcohol, but he was certain that he was delusional.

"Yes! Yes! I understand, Miranda."

"We had a deal, did we not?"

"Yes, but I had no idea…"

The raven paced back and forth across the wooden floor, hopping and occasionally stopping to admire her own feathers and preen.

"Didn't the poem I gave you make you famous? You are recognized when you go out in the street now. You earned money. Your fame grew. I did precisely what I told you I would do. I kept my word to you. And now…I said I would return to you one day and ask a favor."

"But…" The writer put his head in his hands and then leaned his head on his desk. "I had convinced myself it was all a dream. I had convinced myself that you—and the poem—were of my own imaginings. That you were born of cognac and the fretful worries of a writer with a very ill wife."

The raven fluffed her fathers. "Many people convince themselves of lies, Edgar Allan Poe. Many people. From the dawn of time. I consider this part of the human condition. I have no need to lie to myself. But hear me: the truth is that I exist, and I have come to extract my favor. You must hide the Pyramid of Souls. That trunk there, in the corner, should do nicely. Lock the pyramid in there, lock it tight with the key, and then never part with the key until I return for it."

"But I had no idea that I would be safeguarding something from those creatures. What are they?" Poe asked. He lifted his frightened eyes, ringed with dark circles. "They smell wretched. And their faces are leathery. They are the stuff of nightmares. I may never sleep a wink again."

The raven turned her beak toward Poe. "They are soulless. They have aligned themselves with evil. And the Pyramid of Souls is what they covet most. I must go now."

"When will you return?"

"When I can. Until then, safeguard the key, no matter what."

The raven took flight from the open window. As the black bird flew across the star-speckled sky, it cawed, "Nevermore! Nevermore! They are near! They are near! They are near!"

☆   ☆   ☆

Nick sighed and stared at the ceiling. He pulled out the key necklace that had been his mother's. Like Edgar Allan Poe, he had a key and he had secrets. And like Poe, he was exhausted and scared...

Nick didn't remember his mother, Tatyana. Or maybe he did. He was never certain. She had died when he was a baby at the hands of a Shadowkeeper. His father said that they had made it look like she died of a sickness in her brain—that they had done it to make sure they were undetected. Theo's crystal ball had shown Nick the truth. She had died at the hands of Rasputin. The Shadowkeepers were *that* evil.

Damian and Theo had each shown him his mother in small visions in crystal balls. But this confused him, because he never knew if the memories he seemed to have were really *her* or were just what he had been shown of her. Sometimes, he found himself humming a song:

> *Otshi tshornýe, otshi strastnýe,*
> *otshi zhgutshiye i prekrasnýe—*
> *kak lublyu ya vas, kak bayus ya vas!*
> *Znat', uvidel vas ya v nyedobrý tshas.*
>
> *Dark eyes, passionate eyes,*
> *burning and so beautiful eyes—*
> *how I am in love with you, how I am afraid of you!*
> *Since I saw you, I have had no good time.*

He guessed it was a song his mother had sung to him. How else would he know a Russian folk song? But like everything related to her, he didn't know what was real. She was no more flesh and blood to him than the raven inside his crystal ball.

He looked around his bedroom. When he had moved to

the Winter Palace, he was given this room, which had all his mother's things in it. His eyes came to rest on a small gold sculpture of a horse, which was probably his favorite thing since he now rode Maslow. He liked to think maybe his mother knew that one day he would have a golden horse.

Without thinking, he reached for the gold key he wore on the chain around his neck. He often forgot it was even there. It had belonged to her. Sometimes, like now, he would find himself whispering to the key, as if it understood him. And sometimes, the key would warm, as if somehow it *did* really understand.

"Here's the thing," Nick whispered. "I'm starting to like it here. And I don't want anything bad to happen to the family—especially Isabella. So I just need you to help me. Show me somehow that this is really and truly where I belong. Help me live up to my destiny."

The key throbbed against his heart. He rolled over on his side. His head hurt, and that was a bad sign. His headaches were always a sign the Shadowkeepers were reaching out to him. Around him somewhere. When he was younger, a doctor told his dad that Nick suffered from migraines. But now he knew it wasn't that at all. He could sense danger.

His temple throbbed. Nick couldn't explain it, but he didn't think the Shadowkeepers wanted Isabella's essence. After defeating Rasputin in the desert, Nick was pretty sure they wanted *him*. His essence. He was the Gazer. He had tricked Rasputin once before. And he didn't think Rasputin was the forgiving sort.

THE GRAND DUCHESS AND
THE RAVEN

*T*HE NEXT MORNING AT BREAKFAST, THE GRAND DUCHESS was curiously absent. Usually, the entire clan sat down for each meal. After breakfast, but before rehearsal, Nick decided to go check on the Grand Duchess himself. She had become like a grandmother to him. Once a week, without exception, she and Nick had tea together, and she told him stories about her life in Russia, about the family she lost because of Rasputin. She told him stories about his mother sometimes. Mostly, he just liked being with her because she *listened* to him—it often felt as if all Damian and Theo did were bark orders at him or reprimand him.

As he rounded the corner to her private apartment on the top floor, he saw the raven woman walking down the hall, her broad-brimmed hat almost as wide as the hallway itself, her long black dress swooshing behind her like a tail.

Tiptoeing, he followed her, then watched in astonishment as she entered the Grand Duchess's apartment without even knocking.

The Grand Duchess was, in Nick's estimation, ancient. There was no way she could fend off an attack by the raven lady. Nick looked up and down the hall, but no one else was around. He wouldn't have time to alert Theo or Damian or Boris. He ran for the Grand Duchess's door. Usually, he was on his best behavior and best manners around her, but there was no time for that. He turned the handle of her door and burst in.

"Grand Duchess!" he exclaimed.

The old woman looked up, startled, as did the raven lady, who glared at him with eyes the color of coal.

"What an impertinent young man!" the woman in black said, her voice deep and husky, just like that of the raven who spoke to Edgar Allan Poe.

The Grand Duchess smiled. "We were just about to have tea, Kolya—would you care to join us? I have sweets today, biscuits, and Russian tea balls." She pointed at Nick's favorite Russian treat—spherical cookies made with lots of butter and walnuts and rolled in confectioner's sugar.

Nick's mouth watered, but he glared back at the raven lady. "I don't think so."

"Come," the Grand Duchess gently urged. "Come sit and look at the snow. Come reminisce with me, Kolya. Come and meet my friend Miranda."

"Your friend?" Nick didn't budge. The Grand Duchess had known, even as a little girl, that Rasputin was evil. She had an amazing ability to see into the hearts of people. How could she not know the raven woman was a Shadowkeeper?

"Yes. Miranda used to sing opera for my family."

Nick stared at the woman in black. That was impossible. Her face was unlined, whereas the Grand Duchess's face was wrinkled, even though her cheeks were still pink. They couldn't have known each other all those years ago.

"Grand Duchess...can I talk to you alone?" he croaked, his heart pounding.

"Not right now, Kolya, my precious. Later. I'm visiting with an old friend, my child."

Nick's stomach sank to the floor. "Please, Grand Duchess," he pleaded more urgently.

Miranda sat down at the little table by the window. The Grand Duchess's apartment was filled with antiques and heavy Persian rugs. A grandfather clock ticked in a steady, somber rhythm. The snow swirled outside. A howling breeze transformed the swirls of flakes into a blizzard. Staring over her shoulder at Nick, she poured the Grand Duchess a cup of tea from a large silver samovar.

"One lump or two, Grand Duchess?" She smiled at Nick, apparently pleased that the Grand Duchess wasn't listening to him.

"Two, please."

Miranda used her long fingers, like bird talons with pointed nails, to pluck two sugar cubes from a silver dish and added them to the Grand Duchess's tea.

Nick felt queasy.

The Grand Duchess, as she often did, shut her eyes. "I have a memory," she sighed. "I remember Miranda coming to the Winter Palace. My father insisted I stay awake to hear her sing, even though I was so very tired. We dressed in our finest clothes. I remember that my own dress was very much like the one Isabella recently wore for the banquet. And I carried a little fan that had been a gift from a visiting Spanish nobleman."

The Grand Duchess opened her eyes and reached a trembling hand to her teacup. She took a sip, then placed the fragile porcelain with its painting of a gilded peacock back on its saucer. "The evil monk was there," she said. Whenever she spoke of Rasputin, her eyes blazed as if she were a young woman.

"This was shortly before the end," the Grand Duchess continued. She stared out the window mournfully. Rasputin had lied to the Grand Duchess's mother, telling the Tsarina that he could cure her son, who had a terrible sickness. While history books portrayed Rasputin as evil, the truth was even more horrifying. Rasputin was actually a member of Nicholas's clan. But he had turned to the dark side and had become a Shadowkeeper, amassing power through murderous magic. The Grand Duchess spoke again. "I remember that Miranda sang a piece from Igor Stravinsky's *Le Rossignol*."

"*Le* what?" Nick asked.

The Grand Duchess looked at him. "I will have to tell Theo that your education must include the greats of Russian music and not just magic, Kolya. It means *The Nightingale.*"

Nick stole a glance at Miranda. He was still trying to figure out how it was that she had not aged. That could only be Shadowkeeper magic at work...unless he'd somehow misjudged her. How could the Grand Duchess be so blind to it? Miranda was no nightingale. She was a raven. And she was evil.

"I remember being entranced by her singing. It was so special. So magnificent. A soprano, in a tone that could only be described as pure. When she was finished, my father—who by this time was quite depressed—stood and applauded her. He was more animated than I had seen him in months. He invited Miranda to join the family for a late supper."

Miranda nodded. "I believe there was sauerkraut soup."

Nick shook his head. It appeared that his family had been eating all kinds of gross foods for a long, long time.

"Indeed," said the Grand Duchess. "And Miranda came to my side. She warned me about the monk. She told me that I needed to be wary. And she gave me a pendant of a raven with black diamonds for eyes. She told me it was a talisman of good luck. It would protect me."

Nick couldn't believe his ears. "Does Damian know Miranda is here?"

"Indeed, he does," said Miranda. "The family and I—we have known each other forever, it seems."

Nick leaned over to the Grand Duchess and pecked her on the cheek. "Be careful," he whispered.

Then he turned on his heels and left the Grand Duchess's apartment, certain the dark eyes of Miranda were an omen of bad things to come.

For some time, he remained in the hallway, hidden around the corner, ready to enter at a moment's notice if he sensed Miranda was going to harm the duchess. He Gazed into the room but merely saw them chatting over tea. Still, he would not leave the hall until he saw Miranda exit. When she emerged from the Grand Duchess's apartment, Miranda's head was held high. She hummed a song and headed in the opposite direction away from Nick, her black dress swirling like a cloud behind her.

A POINT OF NO RETURN

D URING REHEARSAL, IRINA PORTRAYED A WOMAN EXILED TO Siberia. Dressed in an old, black woolen coat that had patches on the sleeves, with a shawl pulled over her head, she faced into a wind. Alone on the ice of a grayish tundra, she appeared friendless. Then, one by one, polar bears, Siberian tigers, and caribou walked across the stage—which was covered in an eerie permafrost. The orchestra played Shostakovich, which had the rebellious composer's signature motif, a secret code of musical notes he hid within his concertos in defiance of the powerful government at the time.

Eventually, Irina was surrounded by the animals. The music changed, and she danced with the tigers. A polar bear leaped into the circle of big cats and lifted her. Together, the polar bear and Irina performed a *pas de deux*. Symbolically, as she danced, she was less alone, until finally, she was transformed in front of everyone's eyes into an icy princess

Nick watched, as spellbound as the rest of the family. But soon his eyes began to droop from exhaustion. Eventually, despite the spectacle of the new show, he nodded off. He wasn't sure how long he slept, but he was suddenly very aware of Damian's voice.

"Are we disturbing your nap, Kolya?"

Nick sat up with a start. "Nope. I'm just—" And then he realized he had better not finish the sentence. *I'm just so tired because Isabella and I broke into Boris's training room last night and were sword fighting.*

"Well, you, Penelope, and Isabella are due onstage. I hope in between your napping, you have been practicing."

"Of course I have," Nick lied.

He stood in the wings and looked out at the cavernous theater. He took a deep breath, and strode onstage, his footsteps echoing in the emptiness. He found his mark. Isabella and Sascha ran onstage, just as during the other rehearsals. They climbed on Penelope's back. They did everything they were supposed to do. Isabella pirouetted.

And then it was Nick's turn.

He felt a surge rising inside of him, starting with the familiar pins-and-needles feeling in his fingers and a fluttering in his stomach. He pushed the energy out of himself and…Penelope and Isabella disappeared.

"*Ha!*" he cried triumphantly.

"Not bad," Damian said, as he strode across the shining wooden stage. "The best part about the magic in our show is the total lack of props. No sheets or smoke to block the audience's view. No *illusions,* no *mirrors."* He grinned. "They have no idea how we do it. One minute, an elephant is there. The next," Damian snapped his fingers, "she is gone."

"This time, it was so easy," Nick agreed. "I didn't feel Penelope pushing against me at all. It was as if she was lighter than Vlad. It was so easy it was almost…"

All at once, a panicky feeling overcame him. He reached out to hold on to something, but nothing was there and he dropped to his knees. Irina ran to his side. "What is it Kolya? What is it?"

He felt like he couldn't breathe, and he clutched his throat. "It was *too* easy."

"Nonsense," Damian said with a shake of his hair. "You have worked hard. That is what practice accomplishes."

"But I haven't practiced."

"Then you are simply gaining confidence. You are coming into your own as a magician. Now stand up, and bring them back."

Irina helped Nick stagger to his feet, but in his heart, he already knew the outcome. He wouldn't be able to bring them back. He shut his eyes and felt his blood surging through his body. He pulled on Penelope and Isabella, as if racing through space and seizing some sort of invisible magical rope to pull them back to the stage. Only when he pulled, there was nothing there. It was like pulling in a fishing line after feeling a tug on the hook and instead finding nothing—not even seaweed or an old shoe.

"I can't, Damian." He whispered the words.

"Try again," Damian commanded.

Nick looked at him. He saw the shadows beneath his cousin's eyes for the first time, saw how the missing Pyramid of Souls was worrying not just him and Isabella, but everyone. "I know I can't." A wave of nausea rose into his throat.

"No…" Damian said hoarsely.

Nick nodded. "I know I can't get them back. I can't tell you how, but I can't. And it's not *my* magic. It's dark magic." He uttered the words emptily, not from a place of shame, but from a place of grief.

Damian nodded, his face turning white. "They have been stolen from us. By the thief who stole the Pyramid of Souls."

GUARDIAN OF SOULS

*T*HEO!" Damian shouted for his brother.

Theo ran onstage. "Let us go to Sanctuary, see if they are there."

"I'm coming!" Nick said.

"Absolutely not!" said Theo. "I can't let anything happen to you." He put his hands on Nick's shoulders. Theo was one of the bravest men Nick had ever met, but he felt a tremble in his cousin's grip.

"If you don't take me, then I'll come anyway," Nick said. "This is my fault."

"No, it's not. If this is the Pyramid of Souls at work, then perhaps…we should have canceled the convention, the competition, until we knew we had it safe in our hands again."

"If my magic was stronger…" Nick's voice trailed off.

Theo bent over slightly. "Your magic is plenty strong, Kolya." He stood again and glanced at Damian. "We'll bring Nicholai."

"No," Damian shook his head. "*Nyet. Nyet!*"

"You can't make me stay here, Damian," Nick breathed.

"I will cast a spell of stone on you and freeze you right where you are until we return."

"No! Listen to me...! You talk about how the family members have to take care of each other, but now you won't let me come with you?" Nick returned his cousin's glare.

"He's as stubborn as you are, brother," said Theo.

Finally, Damian's expression softened. "Fine. But stay close."

The three of them stood onstage before Theo sent them hurtling through space and time. Sometimes, Nick had nightmares of falling through the sky, so that in his dream, it really *felt* like he was dropping down, hurtling through the air; now he experienced that same sensation in real life. In the time it took to breathe a single breath, they disappeared and reappeared in the desert outside the pyramid. Running awkwardly through the sand, Nick fell but picked himself up in seconds. The three cousins ran into the cool of the pyramid. Immediately, they heard a cacophony of nervous chatter, like crickets and tree frogs.

"What is that?" Nick asked.

But then, in the corridor of the pyramid he could see that the hieroglyphics were moving, twittering, scattering in a crazed panic. They were no longer orderly, but zigged and zagged, bumping into each other.

"What is going on?" he asked one of the hieroglyphics.

"Shadowkeepers," it hissed.

Cautiously, yet swiftly, the three cousins—Nick in the middle, Theo in front, and Damian in the back—turned sideways and slid down the hall into the large chamber.

It was empty…

Except for Sergei.

"Where is everyone?" Theo asked.

"I do not know," said Sergei, who was carrying a large brown paper bag that smelled suspiciously like Chinese takeout. "I got an order from D. B. Cooper for a quart of hot and sour soup, barbecued spare ribs, an order of Peking duck, and fortune cookies—magical ones. I come with the food. He is not here. No one is here. But"—he pointed with his free hand toward a wall of chattering hieroglyphics—"they say that Shadowkeepers were here. They were looking for a little girl and an elephant."

"That little girl was Isabella," said Theo softly.

"She would *hate* that you're calling her a little girl. She'd tell you herself. She's not little," snapped Nick. Fear and anger threatened to choke him.

Sergei dropped the bag of Chinese food, took out a handkerchief, and blew his nose. "I was worried about being paid for the Peking duck! I was worried about the money—

only now I discover Isabella is missing!" He honked into the handkerchief again and dabbed at his eyes. "Who could even eat at a time like this?"

Theo marched over to the wall of hieroglyphics. "Did the Shadowkeeper have the Pyramid of Souls?" he demanded.

The chattering grew louder—a chorus of "Yes, yes, yes, yes!"

Grim-faced, Theo turned around. "We must go home. I don't think the fiends are done yet. Sergei, you come with us. You'll be safer."

Dejectedly, Theo, Damian, Sergei, and Nick vanished from the pyramid. When they returned to the Winter Palace Casino, it was not to the stage that they reappeared, but to Theo's classroom.

"Something isn't right about this," said Theo. "How could the Pyramid of Souls be taken from Jahi?"

"How do the Shadowkeepers take anything?" Nick wondered aloud.

"No. Something is wrong here!" Theo was suddenly like a madman. With crazed eyes, he frantically raced from ball to ball, searching for something.

"What is it?" Nick asked.

Theo touched one ball, then the next, then the next, shaking his head each time. Finally, he came to the largest crystal ball in his collection.

"This one will tell us."

Nick stared at the ball. It was enormous. And it looked familiar. "Is that…?"

Theo nodded. "Yes, it is, Kolya. Behold: P. T. Barnum's crystal ball."

✧ ✧ ✧

Egypt, 331 BC

Alexander the Great strode out of his tent, long hair flowing, his infamous temper flashing. With his long-fingered hands, he grabbed a man in white robes.

"Panos! I want that soul house. Do you understand me? Either you retrieve it for me, or I will sentence you to death—by trampling."

The man shrunk back. "Please…no, I beg you!"

But Alexander would not listen. "You will be trampled to death by my herd of elephants unless you get me that soul house."

The other man pleaded, "You have all the power a man should have!"

"I want the power of the gods!" Alexander bellowed.

"But you are now known as master of the universe. You are known as the king of Asia. In Tyre, you crucified your enemies and sold their children and wives into slavery. No one is more feared, more honored, more revered, more powerful. You command the whole of the world. Is that not enough? Is your appetite for power so enormous that it cannot be filled?"

"How dare you question my power?" Alexander gestured at the two hundred elephants lined up in the distance. "Don't you see? I want to collect the very souls of my enemies even after their deaths. I want to hear their cries of agony. I want to own them for all eternity. Get me that soul house, or face the elephants' stampede."

The man in the white robes fell to his knees and bowed before Alexander. "Oh, great king, please have pity on me."

With an icy voice devoid of any emotion, Alexander said, "The soul house or your life."

Leaving the man prostate on the sand, Alexander strode away, his thighs like sinewy tree trunks.

The man in the white robes remained face down in the sand for many moments. Finally, he stood and walked into his tent. There, on a wooden table, sat the Pyramid of Souls. It was made of gold and shimmered magically, even in the pale light of the tent.

The man wept. "I fear Alexander grows madder by the day. In his hands, this soul house will bring ruin and even more despair."

He sat quietly, as if forging a plan, steeling himself for what lay ahead.

At sundown, he wrapped the soul house in plain cloth, then placed it in a basket woven from reeds. As the sun set over the desert, he peered out of the tent and then scurried past soldiers and guards to the elephants.

"You there!" said one general. "What are you doing?"

"Tending to the elephants."

"We have men for that. We do not need the king's personal magician and soothsayer tending the elephants."

The magician straightened, trying not to betray his fear. "Those are Alexander's wishes. Dare you defy the master of the universe?"

The general looked wary. "All right, then."

"Thank you." The magician hurried past and ran through the desert night to the elephants. They stood in family groups. He touched one elephant, than another, soothing them with his voice. "I have come for the matriarch." Rejecting one after another, carefully stepping between the large beasts, he finally found the elephant he was searching for.

"Please," he said to the elephant. "You must carry me through the desert. I must return to my people with the Pyramid of Souls, and we must ensure that it never falls into the hands of the king. I need a brave elephant—one who is a mother, who understands the fragility of life; one who has children and a family. Such an elephant would understand the need for compassion and not destruction, for a world without war so that children may be brought up to walk as peacemakers. Please. I beg you, wise elephant. Please carry me through the desert!"

The elephant's eyes were, indeed, compassionate and understanding. She lowered her trunk into a perfect "U" and lifted the man onto her back.

With a mournful look at her elephant family, she touched her trunk first to one elephant, then another. She came to her mate. She bowed her head and pressed her forehead to his. Then she started out into the desert on the long trek to safeguard the Pyramid of Souls.

☆　☆　☆

"The elephant…" Nick whispered. "Please tell me that wasn't Penelope. I knew she was ancient, but…the magician must have cast a spell on her so she would live this long."

Theo touched the ball. "What I fool I've been."

"What?" asked Damian.

"The Shadowkeepers didn't want Isabella's soul. She's just a—a bonus. They wanted to capture Penelope. She's the keeper of the Pyramid of Souls. As long as they have her, they can use the pyramid as they wish."

"But," Nick said, "I don't understand."

Damian grabbed Sergei by the arm. "You! You still

smell of Peking duck! You crazy animal dealer, where did you get Penelope?"

Sergei cowered. "Are you going to turn me into a flea on a pig's behind?"

Theo stepped in, speaking more calmly. "No. My brother is not going to do that. But we need to know how you obtained Penelope."

"A man named Anubis approached me and said he had an elephant for sale."

Theo staggered backward. "Sergei, you fool. Did you not check the animal's papers?"

"Papers?" Sergei asked. "Elephants don't come with papers!"

"Well, surely you must have some way of determining if an animal is stolen," Damian spat. "Do you have any idea who Anubis is?"

"An elephant dealer."

"No!" Theo shook his head. "What have you done? Come, we must go to Damian's library!"

Nick followed Theo as he and Damian raced from the classroom and down the hall. "What is it, Theo?"

"The hieroglyphics were the clue all along!"

THE JACKAL

AMIAN'S LIBRARY WAS CRAMMED TO OVERFLOWING WITH books on magic on shelves that rose up every wall to the top of the room. Theo ran to the ladder that took him to the shelves up near the mural-covered ceiling. He pulled an enormous old volume down and descended the ladder in a *whoosh,* finally setting the book on a table.

The cover had hieroglyphics on it. It opened itself, and Theo pointed as pages turned. In the center page, when the pages stopped turning, Nick saw that the volume was filled with the intricate picture-drawings of ancient Egypt.

"This is the oldest book the family owns, from the Library of Alexandria, rescued from its destruction. And this, Sergei—this is Anubis."

Rising from the pages, one of the hieroglyphics formed

into a three-dimensional figure. It had the head of a jackal and the body of a man, and it held a flail and an ankh. Its eyes were dark and piercing.

"He is, in Egyptian symbolism, the protector of the dead," Theo explained. "While his appearance might be frightening, to the Egyptians, he is part of the circle of life, the circle of magic. But over time, Anubis aligned himself with the darker arts."

Nick gulped.

Damian's face was stormy. He whirled toward Sergei, who lurked shamefully in the doorway. "You got the elephant from Anubis? Sergei—you will be a flea on a *flea's* bottom on the rear end of a pig!"

Sergei crept forward and peered at the Anubis in the middle of the book. The jackal bared its teeth, showing its canines. "He did not look like that. How was I to know?" Then a look of horror crossed his face.

"What, Sergei?" Nick asked. "Tell us. Even the smallest detail might help."

"He wore an ankh ring. I can see it in my mind now, clear as my own hand: a gold ring in the shape of an ankh. I am so sorry. So sorry." He brought his hands to his face.

"Sergei," said Theo. "It matters not how this unfortunate turn of events occurred. All that matters is getting Isabella back. Penelope back."

"I still don't understand," Nick said.

"Penelope was the original keeper of the Pyramid of Souls since the time of Alexander. Alexander's soothsayer must have cast a spell over her and charged her with originally safeguarding it. Over time, though, like so many of our relics, the Pyramid of Souls was stolen, changed hands, gambled away. When humans came in contact with our relics, they just saw gold or jewels, not the magical powers contained within the relics. Penelope herself changed hands many times, perhaps hiding her identity as a simple circus elephant. Atsu and Siti's family are her latest keepers, but they did not know her history. They do not have the animal arts in their bloodline. When it was time to come to the convention, they brought the pyramid with them and left the elephant at home, not realizing the extent of the bond between animal and relic."

"And in Rasputin's quest for all the magical artifacts ever forged and created, in his insatiable thirst for power, the time had finally come," Damian continued, his eyes narrowing. "The Shadowkeepers must have seen their chance to steal the pyramid. Anubis must have known all along that if he could separate the elephant from the pyramid, the relic would be especially vulnerable—and if the Pyramid of Souls were in the hands of the Shadowkeepers—he could rule with them in fear and death. He disguised himself, sold the elephant to our ridiculous friend Sergei, and planned his thievery with Maria and Rasputin, no doubt. He did not intend for the ancient elephant to get sold into our family. I am sure when he sold her to Sergei, he thought she would end up in a circus, performing, quite literally, for peanuts. When Maria was in the stalls and saw the elephant, he needed to act."

Nick's eyes widened. "Can Anubis change shape?"

"Of course," said Damian.

"When Maria was here, she had a wolf-life creature with her. But...it wasn't a wolf. It was a *jackal!*"

"We are all in danger until the Pyramid of Souls is returned to the Magickeepers," Theo stated. "And to the elephant."

"We must go find Jahi," Damian added. "He will perhaps know how we can recover it."

"We have to hurry," Nick urged. "What happens to people after they're in the Pyramid of Souls?"

"The longer they remain, the harder it is to retrieve them," Theo replied. "Like those buried with the pharaoh, some souls remain there forever." He closed the book, trapping the hieroglyphics inside. "Let us see what Jahi knows about the Jackal."

The four of them hurried from the library and took the hotel elevator to Jahi's room. He did not answer the door when Damian knocked, so in true Damian fashion, they walked *through* the door.

There, they found Jahi wringing his hands and talking to himself.

"Jahi! Jahi!" Damian shouted. "What is it?"

But the man was in a trance and would not communicate. Nick looked around the room, searching for clues.

He found one.

A raven's feather.

"Theo…I'm going to go find Sascha. She'll be worried."

"Good idea."

Nick left, but instead of going to find Sascha, he scrambled up to his own room. He wanted to Gaze without being under the watchful eyes of his cousins. He found Sascha anyway—she was waiting for him outside his door.

"Hey there," Nick leaned down and hugged his cousin's tiger. He buried his face in Sascha's thick fur. "We'll get her back. I promise you." He could barely speak. His pain over Isabella was like a stone lodged in his throat.

He opened the door to his room and the tiger followed him inside. Nick took a deep breath. *Gaze with a true heart.* That was what Theo always told him. *Gaze without thought for personal gain.* Never had Gazing been so important as that moment.

He touched the key he wore around his neck, as if to conjure the power of his mother. Then he walked to his crystal ball and placed his hands on it, shutting his eyes in concentration and willing a vision to come to him.

"Nick!" He heard Isabella's voice. He opened his eyes. Isabella's face was inside the ball.

"Nick! Theo! Damian! Irina! Penelope and I are trapped!"

Nick touched the ball. "Isabella, don't be afraid. I'm going to come find you!"

As soon as he touched the ball, Isabella's face disappeared. Instead, he saw Rasputin.

"Nicholai Rostov," the monk said in a cruel, mocking voice. "We meet again."

"I *knew* you had to be behind this." Nick glared at the Shadowkeeper.

"Indeed. It's very simple, Nicholai. I will capture the souls of all the people you love. I already have Isabella. Next it will be the Grand Duchess. Irina. Your grandfather. *Theo*. I will take them one by one."

"Why not take me first? Why go after them?"

The monk laughed, his howl cackling and echoing in the room. Sascha reared on her hind legs and roared. Vlad hid his head beneath his tiny paws.

"What would be the fun in that?" Rasputin asked, his mad eyes flashing. "I want you to suffer, Nicholai. I want you to see everyone you love vanish into my possession."

As Nick listened to Rasputin, he realized that the evil monk sounded almost exactly like Alexander the Great. Clearly, the Shadowkeeper lineage extended as far back as the Magickeepers. And no amount of power and suffering was enough for them.

"Why is it that you want me to suffer?" Nick hissed. "What have I ever done to harm you?"

Rasputin leaned forward, his face pressed against the glass. "Do you forget the Eternal Hourglass you stole from me?"

Nick stared at him. There was no use in mentioning Rasputin started this latest conflict. "I don't forget. But...you sent Shadowkeepers to try to kill me."

"Not kill you, persuade you to join us. Nicholai Rostov, it's not what you *have* done. It is what you *will* do."

"I don't understand."

"From the moment you looked in Madame Bogdonovich's crystal ball and could see Egypt, I knew you were the one destined to destroy me once and for all. Damian, Theo... and now you: the *only* Gazer born in this generation. The only one. In that entire convention, do you know that you are the only Gazer other than Theo and Damian? So it's quite simple. I will destroy all you love until you join me—until your bitterness is so all-consuming that you share my hunger for power, and you share my magic."

Nick glared at him. "I'll join you right now, if that's what you want. You just need to release Isabella and Penelope and all the rest of the people you took from Sanctuary."

"A trade."

"Exactly."

"Last time we enacted a trade, you betrayed me. You tricked me. You ended up with the Eternal Hourglass."

"This is an even trade. I will join you if you return the Pyramid of Souls to the Magickeepers."

"And you consider that an even trade?"

"If what you say is true, then don't you?" Nick asked.

The madman laughed. "You strike a hard bargain. But this time, my little Magickeeper, we're going to meet alone. And not in the desert. This time, you will not use trickery to defeat me."

Nick tried to think of someplace in open sight where he could meet Rasputin. He thought of his grandfather and his dad. "Okay. No sand. This time, I will meet you in the center of the Hoover Dam."

"Fine, my friend."

"I am *not* your friend."

"The dam. I will arrive with the Pyramid of Souls. If I see Theo or Damian, I will throw the pyramid into the water, and that will be the end of it. Do you understand me? You may bring the Egyptian twins. Just the children. They can take the Pyramid of Souls home to Egypt, and you will come with me."

"How do I know I can trust you?"

"You don't," Rasputin said menacingly. "Nor do I know if

I can trust you. But I'm your only chance of Isabella surviving, so I suggest you take me up on my offer."

"Yes," Nick said. "It's a deal."

The crystal ball went dark, and Sascha stared up at Nick with pleading eyes.

"I know, I know, Sascha." He sighed. "But what choice do I have?"

A SIGHTSEEING TOUR

S O YOU UNDERSTAND WHY WE HAVE TO KEEP THIS SECRET, right?" Nick asked Atsu and Siti later that evening.

Siti nodded. "Poor Nanu. That is the elephant you call Penelope. We left home weeks ago with the pyramid, and spent time with family in Africa. We did not know Nanu was gone. A spell was cast on our elephant keeper."

"*Nanu*." Nick repeated the name. "That's really nice. What does it mean?"

"'Beautiful,'" said Siti. "She has a beautiful soul."

Atsu said, "Our father is beside himself. He feels responsible. Nanu was kidnapped. The pyramid was stolen. This is all our fault."

"No." Nick shook his head. "Rasputin wants every magic artifact ever forged or created. He can't have too much power.

Just like Alexander the Great. Alexander murdered all his enemies. He enslaved the wives and children of whole cities. Is Rasputin any different? Is his daughter any different?"

None of them spoke for a moment.

"How do we look?" asked Siti finally.

"Like two tourists. What about me?" He peered down at his clothes, which he had bought in the hotel gift shop. The three of them wore Las Vegas T-shirts, sunglasses—even though the sun had set—baseball caps, sneakers, and sweatpants.

"Like an American tourist," said Atsu.

"Now listen." Nick spoke solemnly. "Don't worry about me. You just worry about the Pyramid of Souls."

"But," Siti said, touching his arm, "you are our friend."

"I'll be fine. I have a plan."

"We wish you would tell us, Nick," said Atsu.

"If I do not tell you, then Rasputin cannot ask you or somehow force you to tell. But don't worry."

"Not so easy, my friend," Atsu replied.

The three of them slipped out the front door of the hotel and hurried down the street to one of the other big hotels on the Las Vegas strip. There, they caught the last bus to the Hoover Dam, over an hour away.

Settled in their seats, Nick stared out the window as the sky darkened and stars began to twinkle. Minute by minute, the time gnawed at him. He felt a knot in his gut, but when he thought of Isabella trapped inside the pyramid, he concentrated instead on going over each part of his plan.

The entire ride, Nick, Atsu, and Siti were silent. At one point, Siti took Nick's hand and squeezed it.

"Good is on your side, Nick. You will not fail."

Nick glanced at her. "I hope you're right."

Eventually, the bus slowed and then stopped. The tour guide, who had been prattling on into a microphone about the sights, stood. "Time to disembark. Those who wish to take pictures of the dam at night may do so. Others can walk across the dam. The bus leaves in precisely two hours. I'll remain here so you can ask me any questions. Enjoy one of the engineering wonders of the world!"

Nick, Atsu, and Siti climbed off the bus and milled around with the small crowd. "I don't see him," Nick whispered.

"What if he doesn't come?" Atsu asked.

"He will," Nick replied grimly. "He hates me that much."

"Why?" Siti asked.

In his head, Nick could hear the words he'd despised at first when he'd arrived to live with the family—the words of his cousin Damian, the words he now embraced. "Because of my destiny."

The three of them walked cautiously toward the center of the dam. A forecast of rain, along with a huge cloud cover, meant very few tourists were on the dam that night. The massive expanse of concrete was lit up with spotlights through a haze of fog. Nick could hear the deafening roar of water below them. He knew it was a long, long, long way down.

A mist filled the air, making the night feel humid despite the desert and reducing visibility. Nick scanned the dam, squinting. Finally, on the far side, half a football field's length away, Nick spotted him. He would stand out anywhere. Though he wasn't in his monk's robes, he had matted hair and an unruly beard. He was dressed in black pants and a black shirt. Even from far away, his eyes were piercing. They pulsated with hatred. They called to Nick hypnotically.

"Stand in back of me," Nick told the twins. "When he puts the pyramid down, I'm going to walk toward him. You grab the pyramid. Take it on the bus back to the hotel, and have Damian and Theo free the souls."

"What about you?" Siti's voice trembled.

He met her gaze. "I must meet my destiny."

He walked more quickly, trying to put as much distance as possible between himself and Siti and Atsu to ensure their safety. Enough people had been hurt by the Shadowkeepers over the years. He hoped the twins would follow his plan precisely.

Alone on the dam at last, he came within ten feet of Rasputin. "Where is the Pyramid of Souls?" he asked.

The monk placed a worn leather satchel on the ground. He opened it and took out an object concealed in white linen.

He unwrapped it slowly…and Nick couldn't help but gasp as its triangular point gleamed in the darkness.

"For obvious reasons, I will rewrap it so we do not attract unwanted attention." Rasputin hurriedly covered the ancient artifact again and shoved it back in the satchel.

Nick took three steps closer to the monk. "Atsu?" he called over his shoulder. "Go and get the leather case."

Atsu walked past him cautiously and placed a hand on the satchel handle. Nick took another two steps closer to the monk.

"Return to Siti, Atsu. Then the bus."

His friend appeared to hesitate.

"Atsu…no. Do as I say."

Atsu nodded sadly, lifting the heavy satchel. He moved behind Nick and walked toward his twin sister.

"I see you thought better of trying to trick me again," Rasputin said. "Your cousin will have her life back. And you and I will rule the magic world."

Nick took another step toward the monk. Then he suddenly ran to the edge of the dam. He climbed up the metal railing separating the walkway from thin air.

"What are you doing?" the monk hissed. He made an attempt to grab Nick.

"I'd rather die than end up with you," Nick declared.

And with that, he dove over the edge in a horrifying leap toward the raging waters below.

A ROAR OF WATER

*A*LL ALONG, NICK'S PLAN HAD BEEN TO DIVE OVER THE EDGE and then levitate down the river to safety. But once he was over the edge in the sheer blackness of the misty night, he lost his bearings and found himself plummeting in the direction of the most dangerous part of the water, roiling and foamy and violent. Nick tried to levitate, but it was no use. He had no sense of up or down. The confusion weakened his magic. He fell faster and faster, until the roar was so deafening that he couldn't even hear his own thoughts.

He had always heard that people's lives flashed before their eyes before they died. Now he knew this was so. As water sprayed his face, images swirled through his mind. He saw his grandfather and his father. He saw himself skateboarding. But then he had a rush of memories from the last six months, with the new family he'd never known he had. He saw the smiling faces of his clan of cousins and relatives, he saw the bright lights of the stage, he saw the animals, and he saw his cousin, Isabella—his best friend. Knowing she was going to be safe, he was ready to plunge into the water. He was willing to trade his life for hers.

And then a miracle happened.

Suddenly, Nick fell against something—and it wasn't water. He felt strange creatures beating him in the face. He thought they were bats. Then he was lifted, buoyed higher and higher. He waved his arms, trying to see, but he only faced blackness.

As he was lifted higher, he realized what the creatures were.

Ravens.

Hundreds, if not thousands, of them were holding onto him, flapping their wings and carrying him far from the dam, far from the rushing waters below—and best of all—far from Rasputin.

STARRY, STARRY NIGHT

W HEN NICK REALIZED THE RAVENS WEREN'T HURTING HIM, that they were instead saving his life, he relaxed and allowed himself to be carried through the desert night. The breeze from their wings soothed him, and the sky caressed his face, as if welcoming him back from a watery grave. The rain and cloud cover that had offered him darkness at the dam had blown over, revealing the Milky Way trailing across the sky and a crescent moon.

Eventually, the birds slowed their flight, drifting toward the earth, and Nick was set down in the soft desert sand.

Miranda stood there in the moon's glow, a pleased smile on her unlined face.

Nick faced her. "I don't understand. I—I thought you were on *their* side."

"What did Madame B. tell you the very first time you Gazed?"

Nick thought back to the night of his thirteenth birthday. "She said never assume."

"Precisely."

"But...you—you haunted poor Edgar Allan Poe. He was a mess. Delusional."

"Walk with me, Kolya," Miranda said. The flock of ravens remained behind them, and together Nick and the strange woman strolled through the chilly desert air.

"Edgar Allan Poe was a very disturbed man. Sometimes, Kolya, we use our magic thinking it will do good. I gave him his celebrated poem, hoping it would help him. I chose him because I knew he needed inspiration in order to save his wife. I chose him thinking that his fearlessness as a writer meant he was destined for greatness. Had I known he was so fragile...perhaps I would have made a different choice."

"So all along, you've been a guardian of the Pyramid of Souls?"

She nodded. "Ravens are found in Egypt, you know. My ancestors go as far back as the hieroglyphics, too. And just as Anubis was the protector of the dead as they made a journey to the afterlife, we were the guardians of the Pyramid of Souls. Alexander the Great stole it during his campaign of destruction and despair at the fall of Tyre. Alexander's magician, fearing its power, took it into the desert, intending to bury it. For a time, the elephant was its keeper. Only animals were entrusted with it, because only the animal kingdom is free from greed. But grave robbers obtained it, and as you know, artifacts still get stolen from one side by the other, over and over throughout history."

"So you really *are* a friend to the Grand Duchess."

"Yes. And you really *are* an impudent young man." She winked at him.

"And out in the barn? When Maria was there? All the ravens?"

"I've been watching out for you, Kolya."

"Why?"

"Because I predict great things for you." She smiled ruefully. "I learned my lesson with Edgar Allan Poe. I choose those whose destinies are great...but I choose them more wisely now. I cannot make the weak strong. But a leader—a boy who will grow into a man, shaped by his destiny and a true heart...well, he is one to safeguard as closely as the Pyramid of Souls."

Nick swallowed. "If you hadn't saved me, I would have died at the dam."

"I could not have allowed that to happen."

"I'm really sorry I doubted you. I wish you had told me who you really were—"

"But you needed to see with your heart," she interrupted. "That is the true vision of magic. Never assume, Kolya. See with your heart. Listen with your soul. Now come...I am sure your cousins will be worried sick. And I'm sure you want to see Isabella."

"Will she be all right?"

"Like you, Kolya, she is pure of heart. Even the Shadowkeepers can't turn her from her true self."

As Nick and Miranda returned to the flock of ravens, the birds gathered close to him. Now, instead of being frightened by them, he stretched his arms wide. With a *whoosh,* they lifted him skyward.

"*Whoo!*" Nick let out a huge yelp. Then, facing the starry sky, he was lifted homeward. He was returning to the place he belonged—to his True North.

THERE'S NO PLACE LIKE HOME

ICK WALKED CAUTIOUSLY INTO ISABELLA'S ROOM. THE entire clan was gathered around her. The room was silent, and Nick's heart seemed to plummet to his shoes as he walked.

Sascha was lying in bed with Isabella, and his cousin had her head on Sascha's belly. Isabella's long brown hair was splayed out near her head, and she was pale—he had never seen her so pale.

The crowd around her parted.

Swallowing, but finding his throat was dry, he approached her bed. Her chest barely rose and fell, and he could hardly tell if she was breathing.

"Isabella," he exhaled and knelt by her side. "I'm so sorry. I wish I had never made you disappear."

At the foot of the bed, Sergei was crying and wringing his handkerchief out. He blew his nose. Then he wailed, "*Ohhhhhhhhhhhhhhhh!* What a tragedy! What a tragedy! The horror of it all!"

He continued sniffling. Damian put a hand on Nick's shoulder. Nick stared up at him. "I'm sorry I didn't tell you what I was going to do," he confessed, "but I felt like it was the only way. He said if he saw either you or Theo, he would throw the Pyramid of Souls into the waters."

"Cousin…this time it worked out. But next time, you might not be so lucky."

Nick nodded. Then he turned back to Isabella. *Come on, little cousin, come on!*

Sergei blew his nose again. "It doesn't seem right that in all this, the little girl is the one who gets hurt."

The room was silent. And then they all heard her say, weakly, "I am *not* a little girl."

Nick started laughing.

Even Damian laughed. "Indeed, she isn't!"

Isabella opened her eyes. "We need to rehearse. The competition is the day after tomorrow. And I want to win."

Nick shook his head. "Even after everything…you're still the most competitive person I know."

Even as he teased her, he looked into her eyes. He didn't have to Gaze. It was unspoken: Isabella was back, unchanged.

THE WORLD'S GREATEST MAGICIANS

ACKSTAGE, NICK ACCEPTED A HUG FROM ATSU AND SITI. "LET us not lose touch," Siti whispered. "You have done a great thing. You have returned the pyramid. And our elephant."

Nick flushed slightly. "Anyone would have done what I did."

Atsu shook his head. "No. Not anyone. Come, sister, we must watch Nanu's final performance before bringing her home." He shook Nick's hand. "Until we meet again."

Siti kissed his cheek. "You indeed are as great as your destiny portends. Someday you will lead us all."

After the twins left, Nick watched from the wings. The Parisian clan had a fantastic bit: their alligator grew to forty feet long, then ate one of the magicians whole before transforming into twenty suitcases and being carried off by twenty magicians dressed in flashy suits from the Jazz Age.

There was wild applause.

And then it was Irina's turn.

She stepped onto the desolate tundra, alone, pitiful. By the time she was dancing her *pas de deux* with the polar bear, magicians in the audience were clutching tissues.

It was time for Nick, Isabella, and Penelope to perform their magic. But they had decided, in light of recent events, that they would do something different—something to honor Penelope and Miranda and all their sacrifices to tend the Pyramid of Souls for centuries.

The stage was transformed into a desert. Penelope rode in mightily, her footfalls powerful, with Isabella on her back arms spread wide.

And Nick flew from the farthest reaches of the back of the theater on the wings of hundreds of ravens, who then dropped him on Penelope's back.

As Penelope rose up on her two hind legs, the ravens took flight and circled the theater.

Then Nick whistled for Maslow, who thundered onstage. Nick and Isabella leaped onto Maslow's bare back, and with a wave to Penelope, they took off into the desert.

As Nick cast his spell, the ravens all flapped down onto Penelope's back. The elephant sprouted wings and took flight, before disappearing behind the curtains.

The applause was thunderous.

In fact, it was so loud that Nick could barely hear anything else.

He, Damian, Irina, and Isabella all walked to the front of the curtain and bowed. They held hands, and he felt something special. Like the sensation of the thread he had felt when the raven had tried to make a connection to him, he felt something binding them. Their ties were now as strong as swords forged in the ancient magic fires.

He belonged here. He always had. As if something had been missing his entire nomadic life with his father. Something as powerful as magic and belief.

Then he saw Theo in the wings. His cousin was not as triumphant as the stars on the stage. Nick saw a look of pride but also of great worry. Because Theo the historian always knew.

His family may have won the competition...

But the real battle was still not won.

And for that, Nick would have to live up to his destiny.

The adventure continues in Book Three of
the Magickeepers series

PROLOGUE

Undershaw Estate, Surrey, England, October 28, 1921

H ARRY HOUDINI STEERED HIS PUTTERING CAR DOWN THE long gravel drive. The shroud of overhanging trees felt cave-like, and he squinted toward the stately red brick mansion of Undershaw, looming ahead. Here in the outskirts of the village, darkness fell quickly and the forest bathed the estate in an eerie twilight...befitting the night's activities.

Houdini parked in the drive and stepped out of his vehicle, admiring the peaked roof and countless windows. His friend's home had fourteen bedrooms and perhaps as many fireplaces. He smiled to himself, his feet crunching on the gravel as he walked to the tall wooden door and rang the bell.

A butler answered the door.

"I am here to see Sir Arthur Conan Doyle. I believe he is

expecting me," said the world's most famous magician and escape artist, clutching his hat in his hand.

"Indeed, Mr. Houdini, the others have all assembled. You may follow me, sir."

Houdini stepped into a great foyer with an enormous crystal chandelier then followed behind the butler, his footsteps echoing on the black-and-white checkerboard marble floor. He passed suits of armor, swords crossed on the walls, and stuffed hunting trophies—including a large moose head. Displayed with equal prominence were several framed black-and-white photos of the wildly popular author of the Sherlock Holmes detective series, receiving one honor or another.

At the end of a long hall, Houdini was shown into a cavernous library.

"Mr. Houdini, sir," the butler announced.

"Splendid!" Sir Arthur Conan Doyle cried. He rose from his leather chair by the fireplace, crossing the room in three long strides, handlebar moustache twitching. "Harry, my friend, how are you?"

"Excellent, Arthur, excellent. And you are well?"

"Somewhat. Somewhat..."

Harry Houdini knew his friend had been plagued by depression after the death of his brother, followed by the death of his eldest son, Kingsley—who had passed away from pneumonia after serving in the war.

"I know, Arthur," Houdini murmured. "I understand. After the death of my mother...well, you know how difficult it has been for me as well. Grief...Grief is a strange beast, indeed."

"Tonight, perhaps, we shall speak with Kingsley and with your mother. Let me introduce you to the rest of our guests. You know my wife, Jean."

Houdini nodded to his friend's wife. "Yes, indeed. Hello, Jean."

"And this here is a close family friend, Dr. Robert Shaw, who lives in Hindhead, not two miles away. We are also joined tonight by a dear friend from London, in for a fortnight's visit, Samuel Barker. He's a barrister and an excellent storyteller, I might add."

Harry Houdini greeted each gentleman with a small bow, but his gaze was mostly fixated on the woman in a high-backed chair near his host.

"And of course, our guest of honor," Doyle said. "Mr. Harry Houdini, may I present to you Madame Bogdonovich."

With a sweep of his hand, the author gestured toward the woman draped in velvet clothes, her eyes made up like glittering butterflies. Her fingernails, lacquered with a deep purple, were as long as talons.

"The pleasure, Mr. Houdini, *eez* all mine." She spoke in a husky tone and a thick Russian accent, waving her hand slightly. Gold bracelets encrusted with jewels tinkled from her wrist to her elbow.

Sir Arthur Conan Doyle twirled the end of his mustache. "Madame Bogdonovich is a fortune-teller and spiritualist of international renown. She has read for the crown princes of various nations, and for the tsar and tsarina of Russia. And tonight, she has agreed to look into the great spirit unknown, to speak with our loved ones who have departed."

Harry Houdini narrowed his gaze. He was used to frauds and charlatans. People were often so impressed by his own illusions and escapes that they believed he was capable of anything: speaking to the dead, feats of real magic...as if he'd been granted gifts from some unseen force. He always cast a suspicious eye toward so-called psychics. And he was deeply concerned that his friend, Arthur, was so easily taken in by wild claims of spiritualists. Grief had rendered his friend vulnerable.

"Pleased to meet you, Madame Bogdonovich," he said carefully.

"You may call me Madame B."

"Excellent, Madame B. I shall be watching you very closely during this séance."

She smiled. "Indeed, you will. Your reputation precedes you, Mr. Houdini. You, sir, are a doubter of magic—even as you create your own illusions."

"Ah," Harry Houdini replied, enjoying parrying with her, "but I freely admit to all gathered here that I do, in fact, create illusions. No real magic is involved. I have no claims to the spirit world."

"Then we shall see," Madame B. purred, "if I cannot make a believer of you yet, sir."

"You can try," Houdini replied.

"Come, let us gather around the table," Madame B. said. "Sir Arthur and Mr. Houdini shall be right next to me, at my left hand and right hand. That way"—she batted an eye at Houdini—"you may keep a close watch over me...to see if, as they say, I have something up my sleeve."

The guests gathered around a mahogany table with elaborate claw-foot legs. Harry Houdini took his assigned seat. He immediately ran his hands beneath it, feeling for a false bottom or hidden lever. He studied the room. Books lined shelves from floor to ceiling, but he saw no place for a coconspirator to hide. There was no closet. He also did not believe that Arthur would intentionally deceive him, so he concentrated on Madame B.

Next to her chair, Madame B. had a large black leather satchel nearly four feet high and three feet wide. She opened it and withdrew a candelabrum, followed by a crystal ball and pedestal. She placed them on the table.

"Please, Mrs. Doyle, would you light the candles?"

"Certainly," said Sir Arthur's wife. She rose from her chair and took a long match set from the fireplace mantle. She struck a flame and carefully lit each of the white tapers.

"Now, if you would turn down your lamps. The spirit world prefers the shadows."

Houdini suppressed a grin. Mrs. Doyle turned down the lamps until the room around the table was pitch black, with only the flickering candle flames for light. But soon his grin faded. The mood in the room grew both somber and expectant. Even Houdini, who doubted he could be swayed by the theatrics of so-called psychics, had to admit that something electrifying was in the air.

"Let us join hands," Madame B. said.

Harry Houdini thought he felt a tingle when Madame B. clasped her fingers around his own. But he shook his head and fought to remain impartial. He was determined to expose her as a fraud preying upon his friend.

"I call up the magic world, the world of wonders, the world of my ancestors, the world of the Magickeepers, to speak to us from across the spirit world," she intoned. "I ask that they reveal secrets. These secrets will remove the doubters within our midst, will serve to show them that magic is real."

The room was deathly quiet—as quiet as a graveyard, Houdini mused.

"Breathe as one," Madame B. commanded. "In...out... together...united...in...out."

Houdini heard Shaw, next to him, breathing in unison with Madame B. He glanced across the table. Sir Arthur Conan Doyle's jaw was tightly set, a study in concentration.

Then, in the midst of the darkness of the study, illuminated only by the flickering candles, Harry Houdini saw that the crystal ball Madame B. had set on a pedestal was glowing with a soft milky white haze.

His eyes widened as he stared at it. The ball was perhaps the size of a large grapefruit or a melon perhaps. The gold pedestal on which it sat was inscribed with hieroglyphics.

The glowing grew brighter, and he heard Mrs. Doyle gasp.

"Remain calm," Madame B. intoned.

Houdini stared, baffled. What sort of trickery was this? How was she performing such an illusion, especially since he and Arthur held her hands?

"Ancient Magickeepers, speak to me. Speak through me. You know what answers we seek."

She shut her eyes, and the haze inside the ball turned to smoke, then to faint images. Houdini would have rubbed his eyes was he not so intent on holding Madame B.'s hand.

"It cannot be," he whispered. There inside the ball was a moving picture of him when he was nine years old. He thought his heart might stop. He had never seen such a thing.

"Harry Houdini," Madame B. spoke, "you called yourself the Prince of Air, performing on a trapeze as a young boy. Answer me, was that so?"

"Yes! But surely this cannot be! How did you—"

"Your answer is all that is required," she interrupted, gently but firmly.

Around the table, the other participants in the séance were transfixed. All of them stared intently at the little boy on the trapeze. He performed feat after feat, smiling, clearly reveling in his antics. With a flourish, he flipped off and landed, waving at an unseen person, beaming and grinning.

"There," Madame B. continued, "the Prince of Air waves at his mother, who has since departed this world."

Harry's eyes filled with tears. He remembered. It was exactly as Madame B said: He had been waving at his mother, always his biggest supporter and the person who never failed to cheer him on.

The smoke in the ball grew dark, almost oily. Madame B.'s face paled. "Harry Houdini, mark my words this night… one day, you will come face to face with evil. You must be careful. On Halloween night, years from now, you will be paid a visit. You will know this visitor by his eyes. Fear him. Protect yourself. Or you will die."

Harry felt as if a spider had skittered up his spine. He nodded, his throat dry.

The ball changed color again. Inside was another moving picture; this time it featured a young man. Now the crystal glowed with an incandescent greenish blue.

"It is Kingsley," Sir Arthur Conan Doyle whispered, voice tremulous. He looked at his wife, then at Madame B., then at the ball. "My son is moving his lips. What is he saying?"

"He is with 'Touie.' Do you know this name?"

"That is his mother, my first wife." Doyle's voice caught in his throat. "She passed away," he choked out.

"This, he says, is the anniversary of his death. Is that so, Sir Arthur?"

Doyle nodded, his eyes welling with tears. "I did not tell you, but I...I thought perhaps his spirit might be strongest on this night."

"He says to beware charlatans. To be careful where you place your trust, or your reputation will be ruined."

Sir Arthur Conan Doyle furrowed his brow. "What does that mean?"

"I can only speak what the spirit world allows," Madame B. responded.

The ball flickered, its glow dying. All at once, a magnificent goblet appeared inside it. Now it was Madame B.'s turn to gasp.

"What is it?" Sir Arthur asked.

"Sir Arthur...beware. Beware, my friend. Beware. A goblet may come into your hands. Protect it."

"But...I do not understand."

The ball grew dark, once more seeming to fill with an oily substance before it went completely cold.

Madame B. exhaled deeply. "That is all for tonight, gentlemen. Perhaps we shall try again tomorrow evening. You may turn up the lamps again and extinguish the candles."

Houdini swallowed, unable to move. Madame B. dropped his hand, now moist and clammy.

Sir Arthur Conan Doyle did as he was told. Then he implored Madame B. to tell him more. "I am puzzled by your visions," he said. "Please, if you could explain..."

The woman shook her head. "Magic, my dear Arthur... the magic I see in the ball, is an imprecise science. That is how you can tell a true Magickeeper from a fraud. I do not pretend to know all. I only tell you what I see. I know the goblet I saw is valuable. But I do not know how it will come to cross your path."

Harry Houdini finally composed himself. He turned to Madame B. "May I hold your crystal ball?"

"You may." She lifted the ball from the pedestal and handed it to him.

Houdini was surprised by its weight. He turned it over in his hands. It was perfectly spherical, without flaws. There were no cracks, no marks in its pristine icy surface. There was no secret button. When he peered inside it, he could see nothing. No moving pictures, no smoke, no light.

"You want to see the pedestal now, do you not?" she asked.

"Indeed, I do."

She handed him the gold pedestal. Again, he held it in his hands and turned it upside down, looking for some trick, some ability to recreate the illusion of life within the crystal. But he could find none. He ran his fingers along the hieroglyphics.

"What do these mean, these figures?"

She met his gaze. "Magic is as old as time. Those figures recognize that."

"What say you, Harry, old doubter?" Sir Arthur Conan Doyle boomed, wiping his moist eyes. "I saw my boy in that glass. I saw him clear as day."

Harry nodded, still puzzling. There had to be a trick. There was always a trick.

"I do not know what to say, Sir Arthur," Houdini finally pronounced with a frown. For *if* Madame Bogdonovich had not relied on trickery, then he couldn't help but arrive at a chilling conclusion: She had foretold his death. Evil very well might be closing in around him and his friend. Impossible? Clearly Doyle was convinced. Illusions...those Houdini understood. The work of unseen forces? This was something he had no desire to do battle with.

"Prepare yourself, Monsieur Houdini," Madame B. warned, as if reading his thoughts. "Surprise is a skeptic's greatest foe."

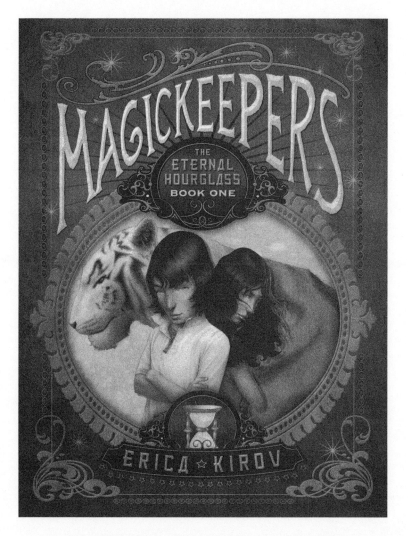

978-1-4022-3855-0 • $7.99 U.S./$9.99 CAN/£4.99 UK

ABOUT THE AUTHOR

ERICA KIROV is an American writer of Russian descent. She lives in Virginia with her family, her menagerie of disobedient dogs, a peculiar hedgehog, a chatty parrot, a kitten named Pumpkin, and a snake. Most days you can find her furiously typing away on her next Magickeepers book. She loves to hear from her readers—you can visit her at www.magickeepers.com, or you can write her at erica@magickeepers.com.